"I Really Should Go Back,"

Abbie whispered.

"No one expects you to."

Her head jerked up. "Why not?"

"Because I told them I was keeping you with me for the night." Her lips parted in protest and he laid his finger against them. "Not tonight, Abbie," he said quietly. "No arguing between us tonight. Nothing will happen that you don't want." He smiled down at her. "Welcome to my world. Forget everything but the essential facts that you are a woman and I am a man and we are here tonight to enjoy ourselves."

Dear Reader:

Silhouette has always tried to give you exactly what you want. When you asked for increased realism, deeper characterization and greater length, we brought you Silhouette Special Editions. When you asked for increased sensuality, we brought you Silhouette Desire. Now you ask for books with the length and depth of Special Editions, the sensuality of Desire, but with something else besides, something that no one else offers. Now we bring you SILHOUETTE INTIMATE MOMENTS, true romance novels, longer than the usual, with all the depth that length requires. More sensuous than the usual, with characters whose maturity matches that sensuality. Books with the ingredient no one else has tapped: excitement.

There is an electricity between two people in love that makes everything they do magic, larger than life—and this is what we bring you in SILHOUETTE INTIMATE MOMENTS. Look for them wherever you buy books.

These books are for the woman who wants more than she has ever had before. These books are for you. As always, we look forward to your comments and suggestions. You can write to me at the address below:

Karen Solem
Editor-in-Chief
Silhouette Books
P.O. Box 769
New York, N.Y. 10019

WindSong

Parris Afton Bonds

Silhouette Intimate Moments
Published by Silhouette Books New York
America's Publisher of Contemporary Romance

Other Silhouette Books by Parris Afton Bonds

Made for Each Other

SILHOUETTE BOOKS, a Simon & Schuster Division of
GULF & WESTERN CORPORATION
1230 Avenue of the Americas, New York, N.Y. 10020

Distributed by Pocket Books

ISBN: 0-671-47130-9

First Silhouette Books printing June, 1983

10 9 8 7 6 5 4 3 2 1

America's Publisher of Contemporary Romance

Printed in the U.S.A.

For Delbert and Elwana Brewster, who taught on the Navajo Indian Reservation, and Lynn DuBose, who lived on the Rosebud Sioux Reservation

Chapter 1

AT THE KAIBETO TRADING POST AN OLD INDIAN, wearing opaque sunglasses and turquoise nuggets suspended by leather thongs from his ears, pumped gas into a 1946 Studebaker. Marshall Lawrence wedged his Ford Bronco bearing the stenciled insignia *Bureau of Indian Affairs Motor Pool* between a battered pickup and a flatbed wagon. The attractive woman next to him glanced curiously at the wagon's rubber tires and he explained, "The Navajo owner whose wagon has rubber tires is uptown. Iron-rimmed wheels signify middle class."

Abbie Dennis smiled, a stunning smile that reminded the Director of the Western Navajo Agency that he had been too long away from metropolitan cities and fashionable women. She looked more twenty-seven than the thirty-seven years her application had stated.

"It seems that I have a lot to learn if I'm to succeed as a teacher out here," she said.

"Don't let the desolation scare you. The Arizona desert kind of grows on you after a while."

Abbie arched a finely winged brow in skepticism.

He grinned, his teeth white against his suntanned face and sun-streaked hair. "It's true. And there are some mighty nice people who live here. I thought I'd introduce you to old Burnett—he owns the trading post—before I run you over to the Indian boarding school."

If the Kaibeto trading post was any indication of the condition of the boarding school, Abbie held out little hope for modern conveniences. The trading post, backed into the lee of a sheer red bluff, was an L-shaped native stone building with a corrugated tin roof and cedar post columns. A round mesquite-staked corral and the gas pumps were the only other man-made structures in sight.

Marshall came around to open the Ford's door, and Abbie gratefully got out to stretch her legs, legs that she had thought too long and gangly in high school. Immediately sand worked its way into her sandals. She ignored the grating beneath her feet and let Marshall, his hand solicitously at her elbow, lead her into the quiet, cool shade of the trading post's porch.

The hinges squeaked as he opened the screen door for her, and the two men inside broke off their conversation at her entrance. She first noted

Burnett because his shock of white hair and drooping mustache stood out against the darkness of the large room. Only when her pupils adjusted to focus on the faded blue eyes of the octogenarian—while Marshall was making the introductions—did she perceive the other man.

The impact of the man's intense gaze almost stunned her.

Actually, she had been aware of him even before the moment that her gaze locked with his. Later she tried to identify that awareness—the kind a mother experiences when she senses that one of her children is into some kind of mischief, the sort a wife feels when her husband's routine actions are subtly altered. But those weren't really good analogies at all. It was a primitive knowledge, as if her mind were a light that had been switched on, connected to a current that flows even though it can't be seen. Whatever, he coalesced within her vision into a dark shape against the myriad rows of canned goods and zinc washtubs, saddles and coal irons.

Jeans that were faded gray at the knees; a navy blue double-breasted shirt; a black felt western hat slung low over the forehead and rolled at the sides; smoldering dark eyes in a shadowed face—these were what she saw.

But the essence of the man—*that* she felt like a blow to her senses. A raw, primeval masculinity that had nothing to do with flesh and blood stood before her. If anything, the man appeared leaner than suburbia's muscle-bound businessman who worked out during lunch breaks at local spas and country clubs and jogged in the evenings along nicely regulated residential streets. In fact, this man seemed not quite as tall as Brad's six-foot-three frame.

Brad—her soon to be ex-husband—belonged in her past, and this man—who in some indefinable way shook the self-containment that had taken her years to build—he certainly did not belong in the future she had planned. Defensively she donned a mask of cool politeness and forced herself to listen to what Marshall was saying. All the while her peripheral gaze took in the silver-banded bracelet inlaid with turquoise, the scuffed cowboy boots, the horsehead buckle on the concho-studded belt wrapped low about narrow hips. She remembered that when curiosity had prompted her to research her new state, she had discovered that the rodeo circuit was big in Arizona, especially in the summer and fall months. A rodeo tramp, she decided scornfully, illogically quite satisfied with her deduction.

When Marshall paused in his introductions, she recollected herself and firmly, crisply, shook hands with the old man. "Glad to have a pretty filly out here, gal," Orville Burnett rasped. "Marshall, son, yer getting better in yer choice of teachers."

Then Marshall was introducing the man. "And this is Cody Strawhand, our lapidary artist whose silversmithing gives Kaibeto its one claim to fame."

A craftsman. Worse by Brad's standards. She

could almost hear his scornful pronouncement: "Society's dropouts."

She extended her hand. For a moment she thought that her hand would simply hang there in space, but then the man took it. Surprise washed over her. The way he pressed his palm against hers rather than clasping her hand . . . it was the Navajo form of greeting about which Marshall had instructed her during their three-hour trip from Flagstaff to Kaibeto. The man was an Indian.

The revelation had little effect on her, but his intense maleness staggered her. True, songs were penned about such encounters, novels written and movies made; she had gone through her teens and even the married years of her twenties daydreaming about such an experience. But she had thought that with the advent of her thirties and what she considered matronly maturity, she had outgrown such an absurd fantasy.

Nevertheless, there she stood, flushing beneath his heavy-lidded regard, short of breath and extremely irritated with her schoolgirl reaction. And slightly frightened. Twenty years of repressing primal, private feelings had not prepared her for this open assault on her sensuality. Unbidden sensations flashed over her that no proper wife and mother was supposed to feel—at least not at thirty-seven. This was another situation that she did not know how to handle.

"Ma'am," Cody Strawhand said with a face as expressionless as a wooden Indian's. Yet she somehow had the feeling that his handshake had been a calculated insult. The nostrils of his thin, bladed nose flared, as if he scented her.

She met his inscrutable gaze with the superior smile she reserved for the more pretentious people she encountered in Philadelphia society. She had learned early how to play its games. "My pleasure, Mr. Strawhand." Her response was about as genuine as the Indian beads in curio stands along the reservation's Highway 89.

After a few more uncomfortable moments of conversation, she escaped the man's dominating presence when Marshall ushered her outside to the Bronco. After the coolness of the trading post, the unbelievably hot August air seemed to suck the moisture from her mouth.

"Are you sure you really want to go through with this?" Marshall asked with a grin.

Expecting an older businessman to meet her at Flagstaff's small airport, she had almost over-looked this trim middle-aged man in khaki slacks and safari jacket. He winked teasingly at her now, adding, "It's not too late to put through a request to the Gallop, New Mexico, headquarters for another assignment."

A moue of feigned despair pouted her lips. "Don't tempt me." Then, in a lighter tone she said, "Why didn't you warn me when you were driving me here what I'd face?"

Marshall grunted as the Ford Bronco lurched over a rock in the dirt road. "I've already warned you that this is the second most isolated post in the nation, Abbie, and that—"

"—that Miss Halliburton will be looking for an excuse to fire me. But I know I can be a good teacher, Marshall—even though I've never used my teacher's degree. I'll prove it to her and the BIA."

"The principal doesn't welcome changes or interference—and especially not from a beautiful, intelligent woman. The teachers don't refer to her as Dragon Lady out of affection. She's a domineering old maid who has a staff of misfits masquerading as teachers. Who else would be foolish enough to work under the conditions we have out here?"

Abbie smiled wryly. "A misfit like myself."

Marshall grinned. "You're one of the least likely misfits I ever saw, Abbie Dennis."

The elite of Philadelphia would probably have said the same. Abbie Dennis had given the best parties, attended the right club luncheons, hosted various civic functions and charity fetes, and been seen at the opera and ballet's opening night galas. She had car-pooled the twins to their football practices and their riding and guitar lessons. She had responded dutifully and warmly to her husband's lovemaking. Abbie, the mother. Abbie, the wife.

But who was Abbie the woman?

The question haunted her. She knew when she looked in the mirror each morning that she faced a stranger. A lovely woman with blond hair skillfully—and expensively—frosted with silver looked back at her, coldly, impersonally. Who was she? Abbie meant to find out.

Kaibeto Wash, a dry creek bed, lent the area its picturesque, postcard appeal. A long, narrow footbridge and a separate bridge wide enough for only one vehicle spanned the deep draw. Abbie held her breath as the Bronco clacked across the vehicle bridge.

"Don't let the dry bed fool you," Marshall warned. "August and September are our monsoon months. At any moment you can expect to see a flash flood boiling down off the mountains beyond through the wash."

So that accounted for the predominance of large deciduous trees on a six-thousand-foot-high desert. There was an old Oldsmobile below, nose down in a loop of the sand-bed wash, that had apparently gotten caught in one of the flash floods. Just looking down made her dizzy.

Once over the bridge, there appeared to be nothing but mile upon mile of red desert, a desert that was broken only by an occasional palisade of mesas or buttes. The stark rock formations resembled prehistoric monsters rising out of a sea of sand. A veritable moonscape—that was Arizona's Kaibeto Plateau.

Plateau. The dictionary had defined it as a relatively level surface raised sharply above adjacent land on at least one side. No heights to worry about, or so she had thought. But with no tall trees to help in gauging distance and size, the flatness was deceptive. Deep canyons, offshoots of the Grand Canyon, split the plateau. Due east of the Kaibeto Boarding School for Indians a high ridge of pale green stratified rock bordered the

horizon for miles until it ended abruptly in a
natural window formation. And to the north
towered the granite dome that was Navajo Mountain.

So much for heights.

The Bronco bounced over another rut and
plunged down the roller-coaster dip. Abbie held
on to the sun-heated metal door and prayed that
the journey would end before the caps on her
front two teeth were jarred loose.

"How much farther?" she asked.

"Just two more miles." At her groan he
laughed. "You'll get used to Kaibeto. And I'll tell
you now, the Kaibeto Boarding School is equal to
the modern facilities at Tuba City."

She recalled passing through Tuba City on the
drive to Kaibeto. It was the office of the Bureau
of Indian Affairs' Western Navajo Agency, where
Marshall was director.

She had been stunned at the squat little town
humped on the broad Kaibeto Plateau—a few
elm trees, old houses of rock built by the Mor-
mons a hundred years before, tar-paper shacks,
and dilapidated stores. Only Marshall's BIA office building, a two-story modern affair of brown
basalt and mirror windows, resembled the civilization she knew. He had told her that the popula-
tion of three thousand Navajos swelled to fifteen
thousand come weekends and Saturday night
when people came in to drink.

She remembered thinking that if Tuba City was
an example of a cosmopolitan Indian town, what
would Kaibeto be like? What had she gotten

herself into? It had been so simple—take the government civil service exam and, presto, she had her first job.

Now she had only to prove her competency as a teacher to Miss Halliburton. She had to! She would fulfill her two year contract no matter how difficult the job at the Kaibeto Boarding School—no matter how deplorable life on the Indian reservation. If only she spoke Navajo.

"I thought there would be some sort of indoctrination," she said, then grabbed the door as the Bronco plunged into a deep gully and careened out of it to crest the next hill. "A workshop of sorts," she finished on a desolate note.

Above a host of faint freckles his gray eyes met hers with laughter before he returned his attention to the obstacle course. "Oh, there was a two-week program—a language-customs project. But the government discovered that teachers adjusted more quickly by being immersed in the Indian culture rather than merely studying it."

"A sink-or-swim affair," she said dryly.

"Exactly," Marshall laughed as he steered the Bronco over the dirt washboarded road that snaked ahead. "Just remember a few simple rules: Don't admire anything that belongs to a Navajo, or he'll feel compelled to give it to you. It's better to make broad statements. Forget about using your camera. It's terribly rude. If you're ever invited to enter a hogan, enter to the left of the firepit. And—"

"And when do I get paid?" she interrupted, laughing.

"I forgot the most important thing, didn't I? Your check will be issued every other Thursday. You can pick it up at the principal's office. And there's a telephone in her office, but it's best to limit your calls to emergencies."

Her eyes swung to his. "No phones?"

"Not in the dormitories. No television or radio, either."

"But the hogans," she accused, pointing to one of the eight-sided homes of adobe and wood that could be detected periodically amidst the camouflaging landscape of sand and here-and-there cedars. The hogan incongruously sported an antenna jutting from its domed roof. "They've got television."

"True. But the Kaibeto Boarding School's too deep in a canyon to receive signals. There are newspapers, if you want to subscribe, though they're delivered by mail a day late."

"Don't offer me another chance to change my mind," she muttered. "I might accept." She felt like crying. Silly of her. A grown woman. Her fingers went to her shoulder bag in a fruitless search for a cigarette before she remembered that she had given up smoking. Sheer lunacy to leave a husband and give up smoking all in one stroke.

"Don't say I didn't warn you," Marshall said.

But she caught his glance of understanding and sympathy . . . and the flicker of male appreciation in the depths of his eyes. That she could handle, *had* handled. But how did one handle this: hot, arid land and furnacelike air that seared the lungs; people who hid behind trees when a car passed rather than let themselves be seen; the total isolation from the rest of the world?

"I know how you feel," Marshall said. "When I first came to Tuba City as the BIA director, I thought it was the end of the world. But in the past seven years I've discovered that people here are real. No plastic facades."

Guiltily she glanced down at her long nails. She was glad now that she had removed the polish. And her false eyelashes. Even her hair was no longer smoothed back in the elegant, intricate knot that many a society matron, who didn't have Abbie's fine bone structure, had tried unsuccessfully to emulate. Now her hair, still its natural champagne shade but three months without a frost job, was caught simply at her nape by a tortoiseshell clasp.

The one vain indulgence that she was unable to give up was her stylish clothing, as demonstrated by her white linen skirt and jacket over a pale blue silk blouse. The other teachers might dress in polyester pantsuits or jeans and dirty sneakers, but her fashionable clothing was her remaining identity with the old Abbie, and she was reluctant to abandon completely that identity.

"It took me a long time to get used to the Navajo reserve," Marshall was saying, "to not being greeted heartily when I visited a Navajo family, until I realized that when a Navajo finally uttered a warm welcome . . . well, he really meant it."

"I wonder if I'll ever get used to the Navajo and this land."

"It's not that isolated, Abbie. Tuba City's just down the road a piece, should you need me."

"Fifty-two miles down the road," she said in a flat voice that echoed the second thoughts that were eroding her initial confident decision to accept the post. "How would I get there?"

"Oh, Kaibeto has a government Jeep of World War II vintage, but you can use it only—"

"—only for emergencies," she finished dryly, and Marshall laughed.

A greater number of Indian hogans, a few of the white man's square houses—maybe a score in total and irregularly placed—and a wire-mesh fence presaged her first glimpse of the boarding school. After a car passed the sign marked *Navajo Indian Reservation* some one hundred miles before Kaibeto, no fences would be seen until this one.

The Kaibeto Indian Boarding School, enclosed by the fence, was built on softly rounded hills. It was more like a campus, with five one-story buildings surrounded by mammoth oaks and cottonwoods and enclosing a playground and basketball court. Marshall proceeded to label the various buildings.

"The larger three buildings are the dormitories. The nearest belongs to the younger girls and boys, the one with the blue shutters to the older boys, and the furthest building to the older girls. There, behind the cottonwoods, is the school, and next to it the cafeteria."

The only other structure was a row of single-story apartments. Some had cars in the drive-

ways, others did not. "Yours is the third one,"
Marshall said.

He took the one suitcase she had brought out of
the rear of the Bronco and handed her the
apartment key. "Abbie?"

She looked up at him, puzzled by the inflection
in his voice. "Yes?"

"Don't let Miss Halliburton intimidate you into
changing your mind."

She was sure that he had been about to say
something else. She smiled. "I don't intimidate
easily, Marshall."

But that wasn't entirely true, she thought, as
she let herself into the empty, bleak apartment.

Cody Strawhand had managed to intimidate
her merely by the sheer force of his masculinity.
His deliberate rudeness had annoyed her, but she
had been even more annoyed at the unsettling
effect his presence seemed to have on her. She
had spent half a lifetime paying for an impulsive
marriage at seventeen to a husband who was
hardly ever home. Another man to complicate
her life was the last thing she needed now.

The hand slid lightly up her calf and Abbie
yelped. The tin can and its crayons, pencils and
scissors clattered onto the tiled floor like a tumul-
tuous hail storm. Two days of teaching first grade
still had not prepared her for the open curiosity
of two hundred fifty-two Navajo children.

But then, a life at the Mount St. Mary on the
Hudson boarding school for the daughters of

celebrities, diplomats and so on, followed by twenty years of marriage to a renowned lawyer, had hardly prepared her for the Kaibeto Indian Reservation.

Could she survive her two-year contract in the primitive desolation of northeastern Arizona? She had to. A thirty-seven-year-old woman with no previous teaching experience had little hope for a position in a normal suburban school system.

At that moment Miss Halliburton, the principal and third-grade teacher, loomed in the doorway. She was a tall, raw-boned woman with a plain face. Though she was in her early fifties, no lines marred her sallow complexion, and no wrinkles rumpled her severely tailored clothing. A mask of powder that never cracked and a pewter gray wig were her two concessions to femininity.

Her eyes, the flat gray-brown shade of stone, glared impatiently. "Well, what happened this time, Mrs. Dennis?"

Abbie glanced down beneath the desk where the boy knelt, watching her solemnly. "Joey Kills the Soldier was feeling my hosiery," she replied with a mortified smile.

"Oh, that." The spinster huffed with exasperation. "You'll just have to get used to it if you intend to stay."

In a rare moment of feminine vanity that overrode her military bearing, Miss Halliburton lifted her hand to pat the synthetic hair that resembled a ball of steel wool. "My first week at

Kaibeto the youngsters kept fingering my curls. Indian children are fascinated with curly or light hair, you know."

Abbie never let on that she knew the woman wore a wig. "I'm finding that out." She recalled her first day when a portrait-perfect Navajo girl, Karen Manygoats, had tentatively stroked Abbie's cascade of tawny gold hair.

The older woman turned to leave, and Abbie said, "Miss Halliburton, just a moment." She rose from her chair and crossed to the door. "It's Robert Tsinnijinnie." She nodded surreptitiously to the eleven-year-old who stood stonily looking out the window toward the massive domed Navajo Mountain that dominated the northern horizon. "He refuses to color with the rest. Even if he doesn't speak English, I know he's old enough to understand it."

From between almost-lashless lids the principal eyed the slender boy. "It's his first year at school. You can spot the first-year children by their G.I. haircuts."

Abbie glanced at Robert, who had not moved from his post by the window. His hair was cropped almost as close as a sheep at shearing time.

"It still isn't necessary to practically shave the child's head," Abbie protested. She was appalled at the impersonal treatment of the children. She could well imagine the indignity the child must have suffered at the haircut, especially at his age.

The woman's knuckles rapped the wall. "What I am trying to impress on you is that there are a lot of procedures you're not going to like or understand, Mrs. Dennis. But you'll just have to get used to them. You can't be a soft touch and survive out here."

Well, wasn't that what Abbie wanted? To find out how capable a person she was? Whether she could survive on her own initiative rather than coast through life as Mrs. Brad Dennis, the lawyer's wife?

But teaching on a Navajo Indian Reservation? She must be reaching senility early. More than likely she would lose whatever identity she had achieved, rather than discover it, in this wilderness of sheep and greasewood that comprised almost a quarter of Arizona and was larger than all of Pennsylvania. She was one-hundred-twenty-five miles from the nearest commercial airport of any size, Pulliam in Flagstaff—one-hundred-and-twenty-five miles of undulating desert.

Yes, she must have lost her mind when she signed the BIA two-year contract.

"You'll just have to learn to adapt, Mrs. Dennis," the principal reiterated before marching from the room.

Despite all her good intentions, despite her resolve to do just that—adapt—Abbie found herself clenching her hands in agitation on Friday when she discovered that lovely, cherubic Karen had impetigo and nothing could be done for the skin infection. Since the school had no clinic, she took Karen across to the children's dormitory, which she knew had an isolation room.

"Are you certain?" she questioned one of the Navajo aides, all of whom had at least a high school diploma. "Only aspirin and antacids?"

The dusky-skinned, lovely young woman nodded her head vigorously, and her ebony hair swished back and forth against the small of her back. "Yes, yes. We are not allowed to give out drugs. We must wait for the weekly visit of the BIA's Public Health doctor."

An hour earlier Dorothy Goldman, the second-grade teacher who only had one year left until retirement, had said the same—and added in a whisper that it wasn't wise to make waves.

"But what happens in an emergency?" Abbie asked the young Indian woman now.

Dalah, clad in jeans and a yellow knit pullover, smiled. Abbie had found herself coming up against that smile often that week—the friendly, blithe smile of teachers and aides who accepted everything as inevitable and right and questioned nothing. "Oh, then it's all right to go into Tuba City. You can use the school's Jeep."

Fifty-two miles to Tuba City! "Give Karen a warm bath and use plenty of soap. I'll be back."

On foot, the three miles to the trading post seemed much longer. Sand crunched inside her open-toed high heels. With sidewalks connecting the various buildings on the school grounds, she had forgotten about the hazard. She would wear something more sensible next time she decided to hike.

Before she reached the footbridge, which was

scarcely wide enough for more than one person, a small dust devil danced across her path, pelting her eyes with sand and whipping her jersey dress high about her thighs. Eyes squinted against the sand and hands fighting her whirling skirts, she stepped out onto the bridge. It shuddered beneath the force of the wind. Modesty abandoned, she grabbed hold of the railing. Her gaze dropped to the wash far below, and vertigo seized her. The knuckles of the hand that clutched the railing turned white.

The dust devil spun on past, but she couldn't relinquish her grip on the railing. She felt that she would never make it to the other side. Then a hand grasped her wrist, and browned fingers gently pried loose her grip. Her gaze spiraled up to encounter the impersonal gaze of the Navajo she had met her first day at Kaibeto. "I'll walk you across the bridge, Mrs. Dennis."

"Thank you . . . Mr. Strawhand," she managed. She walked just in front of him, grateful for the reassuring firmness of his hold on her upper arm and terribly aware of his presence in every nerve cell of her body. Once she reached the bridge's end, she steadied herself with a deep breath and turned to him. Why did the sun seem so blasted hot? Perspiration beaded her upper lip. "I feel so silly, clinging like a scared child to that railing."

"Only children have the right to be afraid?" he asked.

She blinked, unprepared for such a direct remark. In Philadelphia a man would have made some superficial reply. Brad would have said that she did look pretty silly.

Cody Strawhand didn't wear a hat this time; instead, he had the typical Navajo's red bandana wrapped about his wide forehead. She noted that his dark leather-colored hair glinted in the sun with streaks of honeyed brown.

Now that she had the courage to look him fully in the face, she was surprised to see that he had few of the features characteristic of the Navajo children she taught. Oh, he shared the deep-set eyes, the high-ridged bones over hollowed cheeks, the generous curve of the lips—though all of these features were stamped in a harder cast. However, many an Anglo possessed those same characteristics. And Cody Strawhand's eyes, flanked by a network of faint sun-wrinkles, were dark brown flecked with green the shade of the junipers, not the flat black of Indian eyes.

She felt unaccountably threatened by this over-powering virility and the way he seemed to see through to her innermost thoughts, perceiving even her fear of heights. She brought a distant, aloof smile to her lips. "I've never thought about it—fear not being solely a child's right."

He released her arm. "The word 'right'—it belongs to the Anglo."

The sudden inflection in his voice would have frozen a flame. "I—I don't understand," she said.

"The sun—the wind—the water. They are gifts. Not rights. The white man came brandishing paper—deeds of title—his right to the land."

She almost countered with the fact that that had happened centuries ago—that it was futile to argue the point now. And absurd. Then she realized that the discussion had nothing to do with Anglo versus Indian. The man simply wished to put her on the defensive. Obviously, he felt as at odds with her as she was with him.

She made her own voice inordinately polite. "But then, if I understand my anthropology correctly, Mr. Strawhand, the Apache and Navajo haven't been here since Creation either. They wrested the land from primitive and gentle basketmakers, the Anasazi—the Ancient Ones."

"A moot point." He smiled, a smile that did not reach his intelligent eyes, a smile that she somehow sensed challenged her as a woman. "You were on your way to the trading post?"

The swift change from enigmatic Indian to urbane gentleman threw her. A Machiavellian tactic, she was sure. She found herself talking rapidly to cover her disconcertedness as she fell into step with him. His long legs ate up the ground between the bridge and the trading post. "I was hoping that Mr. Burnett might have something for impetigo. One of the children, Karen Many Goats, has come down with it, and the dormitory isolation room, incredibly, has nothing for it."

"Yes, incredible, isn't it?" he said flatly. "Yet the BIA finds budget allotments for computer scientists and manpower development specialists."

His voice had a deep resonant quality, the kind

that hinted at intrigue, captivating the listener—
the kind that storytellers through the ages have
possessed. She wanted to listen to that voice
further, but at the trading post's porch he left her
without a word and swung up into the cab of a
rusted green pickup. Dust clouded the air once
more as he backed the pickup away and took off
down a dirt road that wound back into the
canyon.

"Well!" Abbie breathed, pushing open the
screen door. "If that isn't an Indian for you!"

"Cockamamy!" Orville Burnett said from behind the counter. With his chaotic mop of white
hair over wise, mournful eyes and his rumpled
shirt and baggy pants, he looked like a cross
between Albert Einstein and Mark Twain.

"What?"

"Cody. He's barely an eighth Indian—that's
how Indian blood is measured, in eighths."

"Then why does he live here, like an Indian?"

Old Burnett shrugged and reached for some of
the chewing tobacco that filled a tobacco tin
nailed to the front of the counter. "Guess that's
what Cody prefers. His father, a Navajo code
talker during the Second World War, had only
two-eighths Indian blood. After Chase Strawhand
was elected governor—"

"I remember coming across something about
that." It had been just after she had accepted the
job at Kaibeto, when she had been reading everything she could get her hands on about the
Southwest.

"Yep, Chase Strawhand—first Indian governor

of New Mexico." Orville dipped the tobacco flakes behind his lower lip. "Anyway, Chase married a young white woman. A New Mexico senator's daughter—and by all accounts a blonde, good-looker like yourself."

She smiled. "I take that as a compliment. Do Cody Strawhand's parents live on the reservation?"

"Nope. At least, not Cody's mother." Orville turned to heft a bag of sugar onto the shelf behind him. "Course, Cody never says nothing about his family. Only that he has mongrel blood. No doubt mixed with some French trapper from way back."

Orville turned around and splayed his gnarled hands on the counter that was grooved with initials and stained with age. "I see you've lasted the week now. You might just have the grit it takes to buck old lady Halliburton."

"Not me," she laughed. "I just want to be a competent teacher, not reform the whole boarding school system. I need this job too badly."

She purchased a box of bicarbonate of soda. It was the only home remedy she could think of that might halt the spread of impetigo. Little Karen's face was too adorable to be blotched with suppurating sores. Her concern for Karen Many Goats lured her thoughts back to Cody Strawhand. She wished that she could stop thinking about him.

Still, even as she prepared for bed that night, she continued to think of him. Brushing out her hair, she wandered from the bedroom back to the combined living room and dining room, trying to divert her thoughts in other directions.

Brad would have filed for divorce by now.

Her kitchen was a small rectangular box, but perfect for her.

Had Jason and Justin made the university's football squad this year?

The furniture, a blend of contemporary and Indian design, was shabby, no doubt secondhand. But then, she no longer had to concern herself with impressing Brad's friends and clients, did she?

The twins were as bad at writing as she was. She really must get a letter off to them.

Had Dalah put the baking soda paste on Karen as she had instructed?

Did the young Indian woman and the other aides help the children say their prayers when they tucked them into their bunk beds? Abbie thought of all the nights she had knelt before the boys' beds. Sometimes Brad would come in and stand beside them. But never did he kneel . . . as if the act of kneeling threatened his ego.

Oh, those twins' prayers! They had provided precious moments of reflection and amusement— and closeness. But that period was behind her, and she didn't miss it as much as she had thought she would. She felt as if she had been wrapped in a chrysalis for twenty years, had been waiting for something, some act of nature, to release her.

Cody, if he had been born at the end of the war, would be her age, or maybe thirty-eight. The thought pleased her.

Really, she must stop thinking about Cody. She hadn't escaped her subservience to one man just to strangle herself in an involvement with another. She wanted to be on her own, to answer to no one but herself. This was her chance. Thirty-seven wasn't too late to begin life again, was it? She would *not* think of him.

Was he married—with several wives, as was the Navajo custom?

Chapter 2

"THAT'S VERY GOOD."

Robert Tsinnijinnie looked at Abbie blankly, as if he didn't understand a word she said. But she knew better now. That second week she had finally coaxed him from his post at the window to sit before the long, low table. At eleven, he dwarfed the chair. He was older than most of the boys in the first grade class, but that wasn't unusual.

The Navajo Tribal Council had decreed that a child could continue through the eighth grade, which was the mandatory minimum grade level, until the child reached eighteen. Mostly girls attended the boarding school, because parents needed their sons to tend the sheep. Sometimes a boy went for one year and his brother the next, alternating every other year.

Abbie bent to study the boy's drawing of an Indian shepherd on horseback following his sheep across a desert. Invariably Robert's drawings showed Navajo Mountain in the background. She had noted that all the Navajo children seemed to have a sharp eye for detail. Robert's crayon picture even showed the tracks made by the horse's hooves in the red sand.

Always the red landscape. Later, during recess, she commented on this to Dorothy Goldman.

"Oh, yes," the plump and dowdy old woman chuckled. "Red sand for the red man. The Indian says that the Great Spirit undercooked the white man, overcooked the black man, but the red man he cooked just right!"

Abbie smiled. The Indians had a great sense of humor, which she was just beginning to appreciate. Her gaze swept over the laughing children on the playground. They still had not accepted her, but their aloofness was giving way to a cautious reserve. If only she could speak the Navajo language a little. As it was, they spoke little or no English, and she felt that she faced double the problems of an average first grade teacher.

All the Kaibeto teachers faced unusual problems, but then, maybe the teachers were unusual. Misfits, as Marshall had facetiously commented?

There was the wasted-looking forty-year-old woman who had kicked her tranquilizer habit but had been unable to convince the Denver school

board. There was the young black teacher—he
had been unable to find a job in a small, all-
Hispanic Texas community. And Linda McNabb,
unmarried and a mother. Even in such a liberated
era, the Baltimore school system had refused to
hire the pregnant woman two years earlier. The
BIA, desperate for teachers, hadn't. Redheaded
Linda was enthusiastic about being able to keep
her toddler on the school grounds with her and
have an Indian woman for a nurse, since the
Indians were noted for their love of children.

As she watched the children play during recess,
Abbie thought that she herself was one of those
misfits. But would she ever find out where she did
fit?

Karen Many Goats, her impetigo already fad-
ing, gave a war whoop as she swished down the
slide. And Joey Kills the Soldier pushed three
other children on the merry-go-round—his stage-
coach, he had told her the day before. Beyond, on
the basketball court that was cracked like a jigsaw
puzzle, the older boys were already practicing for
their first intertribal game.

Abbie was on duty for the thirty-minute recess,
and an uneasiness assailed her as her gaze
scanned the playground. Four or five more times
her gaze swept over the raucous children before
she realized what it was that bothered her. Robert
was no longer out there. She crossed over to
another teacher, a recent graduate of Brigham
Young University, who was off duty that period.

"Did you see Robert Tsinnijinnie leave?" she
asked Becky Radley.

Becky looked up from the letter she was writing to her new boyfriend, a lumberjack in Flagstaff. "Uh-uh," she replied vaguely.

Abbie tried to contain her exasperation. The young woman showed far less interest in the children than she did in young men.

I'm definitely approaching old age, Abbie thought. Or was I ever that uninhibited? Maybe that was my problem, why I couldn't be as free-thinking as Brad wanted. Maybe that explained the rumors of his interest in an eighteen-year-old waitress at the Philadelphia Lawyer's Club. Eighteen. The same age as the twins. Becky, for that matter, wasn't much older.

Abbie shook off the intruding thoughts. "Could Robert have gone for a drink of water?"

Becky plucked at an oily lock of mud brown hair. "Gee, I don't know. I didn't see—"

Abbie whirled and went back to the classroom. Empty. Robert's picture of Navajo Mountain still lay on the table. She started down the hallway, looking in the vacant classrooms. The heels of her sandals clicked on the tile, echoing up and down the green-tinted hall. Maybe the dormitory. She found Dalah in the linen room, shoving an arm-load of sheets into the mouth of the monstrous dryer.

"No, I haven't seen him," the young Indian girl said. She clacked the dryer door shut and straightened, shoving back the curtain of ebony hair that had fallen over her shoulder. "He could have run away. Often the children go back home."

"How far away does he live?"

A frown etched Dalah's lovely features as she tried to remember. "Too far," she said at last. "His father is a migrant worker somewhere in California."

"Do you have any idea where he might go?" Abbie demanded.

"Well, he seems to be interested in silversmithing. He once came to Cody's house when I . . ." Dalah blushed.

Abbie guessed the rest—and was surprised that Cody's amorous interest in the attractive Indian girl should nettle her. "How far away does Cody live?"

Dalah pursed her lips in the Navajo fashion. "Oh, just beyond the trading post, maybe a mile or so back up the canyon draw—in the old Spanish mission."

Abbie sighed. To the Navajo, a mile or so could be a block or nine miles. It all depended on how far the lips and chin jutted. And that was something Abbie had not learned to judge yet. She could use the government Jeep—this *was* an emergency—but she didn't know how to drive a stick-shift vehicle. Besides, she didn't dare alert Miss Halliburton unless it was necessary. Losing a child was not the way to start a successful teaching career.

Abbie didn't even consider the old wagon and the two burros corralled behind the Jeep's shed as possible transportation. The school sometimes used the wagon for outings, but Abbie had never hitched up a burro. She doubted if she knew a harness from a hackamore.

She had gone no more than five hundred yards down the road when she gave up and took off her high-heeled sandals. Her hose would be ruined, but the sand wedged between the leather and her toes had abraded her skin unmercifully. Sandals in hand, she stopped in at the trading post, hoping that Robert might have come there. She found Orville back in the pawn room. Like all trading post owners, he kept a pawn room where the Navajos traded their jewelry for credit. Turquoise and silver ornaments, tagged with the owner's name, were mounted all over the walls.

Orville draped a heavy squash-blossom necklace over a hook and shook his shaggy head. "Nope, haven't seen the little devil."

Abbie thanked him and set out again, following the dirt road that paralleled the bend of the cliff on one side and Kaibeto Wash on the other. Ahead in the distance rose Navajo Mountain, which was actually in the state of Utah. Dalah had told her that the Navajo believed that when you died your spirit would go to the sacred mountain.

Though rain clouds squalled now over Navajo Mountain, her bronze silk sheath clung to her waist and breasts where she was freely perspiring. The sandals seemed to weigh twenty-five pounds. A mile or so turned out, she figured, to be two and a half miles. She sighted the rusted green pickup parked next to a mesquite-palisaded corral before she did the mission. In the corral an Appaloosa eyed her suspiciously.

The Jesuit padres had built the mission where the draw angled up to the north, creating an expanse of greasewood-studded plateau. Large, shady olive and fig trees, which the padres must have planted, belted the mission. No large cross topped the pink-tiled roof, but the ochre-plastered bell tower still housed a copper bell that rang irregularly with the breeze.

Abbie approached the massive, open, hand-carved double doors. She found it incongruous that she should feel a natural reverence toward the abandoned place of worship, when the man who lived there obviously carried on his affairs of passion without any consideration for religious desecration.

"Hello?" she called out. No answer.

She stepped inside the outer room. It was like stepping into a refrigerator. The adobe tiles cooled her aching feet. When her pupils adjusted to the dim interior, she found not the barnyard condition that she had expected of a pariah like Cody Strawhand but a well-planned though sparsely decorated room. It was dominated by masculine furniture of good quality. The man was obviously not a starving artist.

The randomly hung paintings above the rust-and-salmon-splashed sofa captured her interest. Vivid colors and strokes—scenes of southwestern landscape, weathered Indians and cowpunchers, maverick cattle and grazing sheep—leaped out at her. She inspected the paintings more closely. The name in the bottom right-hand corner was Deborah Strawhand. His wife? One of his wives?

Feeling like an intruder, she stepped to the

room's far end and called out again. What if he were asleep—or, worse, otherwise occupied in bed? A flush of heat swept over her and she swore silently. Her imagination had to be as vivid as those paintings! Still, she couldn't help but wonder what it would be like to be kissed by Cody. Different. Exciting? Yes, damn it. Funny, she couldn't begin to imagine anything further— going to bed with him. Brad had been the only man she had ever given herself to.

Hesitantly, she followed an arched corridor that opened into a courtyard. Then, from beyond the flagstoned well where a clapboard building formed the fourth wall of the courtyard, she heard a steady thudding. Curious, she moved along the shaded portico that rimmed the courtyard. At the door to the dingy gray frame building a blast of heat hit her. Inside the pegs hung with saddles and reins indicated that the place must have once been a carriage house.

Before an anvil Cody, naked to the waist, wielded a hammer. A leather apron was tied over his faded jeans. The reflection of the forge's blaze flickered across the copper flesh of his torso. Sweat sheened his skin and ran down the channels where his tendons and muscles and ligaments came together, then separated, with each lithe movement of his chest and arms. A swath of hair fell over the red bandana knotted about his forehead.

She stood transfixed, awed by the man's beauty. Her heart seemed to pound in tempo with the thud of his hammer against the silver bar. Then after a moment it seemed she forgot how to breathe altogether.

Cody lifted his forearm to wipe it across the flannel headband and halted in mid-action. His dark eyes locked with hers, and embarrassment washed over her. He couldn't have failed to see the open admiration in her gaze. Only then did she notice the boy who silently watched at his side. Robert. A sigh of relief expanded her air-starved lungs.

Cody laid aside the hammer and wiped his hands on the back of his soot-smudged jeans. During this time his gaze never wavered from hers. When at last he crossed to her, she was able to collect her scattered wits. Had she not faced too many dignitaries to let this single man bemuse her?

"Yes?" he asked.

She nodded toward Robert. Not a flicker of fear showed in the boy's face. "Robert—he ran off from school. I've come for him."

Purposely Cody let his gaze move insolently from her eyes—breathtaking eyes, but a frosty blue at that moment—down to her breasts. They were full and round with feminine maturity. And decidedly sensual with the sweat-dampened silk clinging to pouting nipples. He clamped down the urge that stiffened his jeans. He had had enough of her kind of woman.

The chic sorority girls at Arizona State University, later the sophisticated socialites who had more interest in him than merely being a patron of the arts, who appreciated more than his jewelry. To them he was an Indian and thus different. And that made the Anglo women want him. It amused him that they found his Indian blood intriguing when he was seven-eighths white.

And then there was his mother, the Anglo who had abandoned him—a woman much like the lovely one before him. Strikingly blond, obviously wealthy, undoubtedly spoiled. And with a brittle veneer that would crack under pressure.

He said as much. Bluntly. "Aren't you, too, running away from yourself? Why don't you hightail your pretty, expensive tush back wherever you came from and face your mid-life crisis there instead of taking it out on Indian children?"

She blanched, and he prepared himself for the inevitable slap of a scorned woman. But a slow smile—a dazzling smile—formed faint creases in her otherwise smooth complexion, a complexion as creamy as his was bronze. A slight flicker of admiration for her composure and self-restraint registered on his mental scorecard.

"Mr. Strawhand," she said stiffly, "my concern is for the children, not my feminine libido."

He saw her eyes, eyes as blue as the sky in a second-grader's coloring book, widen at her mistaken choice of words. A lopsided grin eased his harsh features. "Is libido a Freudian slip, Mrs. Dennis?"

At the vulnerable look that suddenly replaced her frigid gaze, he was almost sorry for his sarcasm. But her socialite's mask quickly slipped back into place. "Hardly. Only the truth, which I doubt you would recognize. The truth is, I suspect that you are also running, Mr. Strawhand."

She waved her hand in a gesture disdainful of their surroundings. "You're afraid to face society's demands, so you hide out here, don't you? Play-acting at being a craftsman."

He wanted to wipe the supercilious smile from her face, to grab her to him and kiss away the haughtiness that iced her expression. He promised himself that he would if she ever so much as crossed his threshold again. He would play the role of the savage Indian to her affronted maiden.

His lips formed a mocking smile. "Since communication on any level but the most superficial appears impossible, I will address myself to the problem of Robert. Some Indian children adapt wonderfully to boarding school life. Others are desperately miserable away from their families and never adapt. Robert tells me that he's worked in the fields alongside his father since he was almost four. He misses him terribly. When you take Robert back with you, don't punish—"

"I would never do that," she protested.

"*They* do. Indian boarding schools use forms of discipline that are dehumanizing. I won't traumatize you with the details. Suffice it to say that Miss Halliburton, at least, relies only on a good, swift willow switch for the more difficult children. But with some—like Robert—that won't work. Patience"—he shrugged—"and even then I couldn't guarantee your rate of success."

Before she could protest he took her shoes from her and knelt before her. One hand firmly grasped her ankle and lifted. Involuntarily she caught his shoulder for balance while he slid her left foot into the high-heeled sandal. His flesh was warm beneath her touch. She repressed the desire to stroke the velvety skin. His dark hair brushed tantalizing near the hem of her skirt. She thought of the runs that were probably ruining her hosiery and wanted to cringe.

How like her, Brad would have said. How practical she had been in the face of what should have been wild, uninhibited lovemaking. She had often wanted to cry out that it wasn't her fault, that she couldn't help the direction of her wandering thoughts.

Frigid. Such a repulsive word.

"Keep to the rim of the wash," Cody said as he slipped her other foot into its shoe. "The rain has washed the banks smooth of pebbles there and packed the sand."

He stood, and she looked up into his inscrutable face. "Thank you." The words were almost inaudible.

"Walk in beauty." It was the ancient Navajo form of a combination blessing and farewell. He turned then to Robert, who had never moved throughout the verbal sparring, and nodded curtly at the boy. Like a puppet whose strings had

been released, Robert moved forward to join
Abbie.

She escaped out into the sunlight with the boy,
escaped the sensual enthrallment that had held
her Cody Strawhand's captive.

But Robert had no intentions of letting her
"walk in beauty." When the two of them reached
the bridge, the boy would not budge. She wasn't
particularly happy about crossing the bridge either, but for a different reason. She faced him.
"I'm thirty-seven and you're eleven," she said,
doubting if he understood her, "and I'm not going
to let a child win this battle." She pointed in the
direction of the school. "Now march."

Robert's black eyes glared at her; then suddenly he spit at her feet. Shocked, Abbie looked
down at the spittle that formed a minute puddle in
the sand. In a flash of a second the sand absorbed
it. She looked up at the boy. His face was as blank
as a blackboard. Clenching her fists, she controlled her desire to punch the brat. "You little
beast," she said, smiling.

He blinked, unable to hide his wariness. Her
hand shot out to grab his ear in a secure hold. So
much for the patience Cody had advised using
with the boy. The wrestling hold had served her
well when dealing with Jason and Justin. She
jerked upward and pulled him along with her
across the bridge. He tried to dig in his feet and
pull away, but she only squeezed tighter. Once
she reached the dormitory, she let go.

"Every time you run away, I'll come and get

you," she warned. "And the other children will laugh at you for being pulled along like a sheep by the horns."

She didn't know if he understood the words, but the flicker in his eyes at her next words betrayed his comprehension of the idea, at least. "Walk in beauty, Robert Tsinnijinnie," she snapped and, turning on her heel, left.

Chapter 3

ABBIE HESITATED OVER THE LIST. PERFUME WASN'T among the basic personal articles printed out on the Teacher's Order Form. Following the grocery heading with its itemized canned goods, meats and dairy products, there came the "personal articles"—toothpaste, hair spray, deodorant. But no listing for perfume. And she had used the last of her expensive stock for the rewards.

She smiled, thinking how well the inducement to learn English words was working out. The children were intrigued with the fragrant spray. And Leo Her Many Horses, who most enjoyed smelling the delightful odor that strangely drifted from the glass bottle, had already mastered so many of the elementary words that she thought he might soon be ready to try a reading primer.

Boldly she penned in the name of an inexpensive brand of perfume—all that she could afford now. She only hoped that it could be purchased in the Tuba City drugstore, though she doubted that any store in the small Navajo town carried luxury items like perfume, rouge or fingernail polish and remover, which Joey Kills the Soldier called "eraser."

Abbie wished that she could go into Tuba City herself. Oh, just to eat a hot fudge sundae at the local ice cream parlor! She hoped that she would have enough money saved to purchase a car when her two-week vacation came at the end of the school term, seven months away. As it was, staying in the apartment on the weekends was driving her bonkers. She had completed all her correspondence and read all the back issues of *Town & Country* that had finally caught up with her at her new address.

Earlier that week Becky had grudgingly offered her a ride into Flagstaff when she went to visit her lumberjack, but Abbie had demurred. Flagstaff. Gateway to the Grand Canyon. Suddenly the college town with its tourist and lumber industries seemed like a large metropolitan city in comparison to the isolation of the Kaibeto Boarding School. Next time Becky offered her a lift into Flagstaff, she would accept.

Wistfully, she placed the order form in the appropriate box on the office counter and left the school building. As she crossed the grounds toward her apartment, a voice hailed her. She turned to see Marshall Lawrence striding across the grassless yard toward her. "Dr. Livingston, I presume," he said, his gray eyes crinkling with laughter.

She smiled. "I do feel like I've been lost from civilization, Marshall." How nice, how handsome, he looked in a kelly green sports shirt with epaulettes on the shoulders. She recognized the brand. She used to buy them for Brad. Now he would have to do his own shopping. "I'm on my way back to the apartment. All I want is to get out of my shoes and dress and prop my feet up."

Marshall shook a cigarette out of its pack, saying, "You know, in that dress you could easily pass for a Paris model." He feigned a wicked leer. "Or out of it."

She looked down at the toast-colored crepe with its frothy neckline. Was she indeed still an attractive woman? The encounter with Cody the week before, his dispassionate reserve, had left her wondering just how attractive she really was. Without the mask of cosmetics, was a woman really there?

That encounter had shaken her. That night, after her bath, she had looked in the mirror. Cool blue eyes, her best feature really. Well-shaped lips with an indentation in the center that Brad had once told her was an indication of a sensual nature. How wrong it seemed he had been. Good cheekbones. And the rest of her? She had stepped back. Hesitantly her hands had come up to cup her breasts. Still high and firm. The waist—small; the legs long and slender, without any orange-peel dimples to mar them. Her hands had slipped down to her stomach. Still flat, despite carrying the twins, but streaked with stretch marks, faint now after all those years.

The pungent odor of the cigarette brought her back to the man before her. Now, what had set off that line of reverie? . . . Oh, yes, Cody Strawhand.

"I think I could use a cigarette," she told Marshall. "I'm making lots of adjustments here, but it appears that sacrificing smoking is not going to be one of them."

She tipped her head to his lighter, and he said, "I hope you won't reconsider when it comes time to renew your contract, Abbie." He fell into step with her. "I'm counting on seeing you for a long time to come."

She exhaled slowly, savoring the pleasure. Her first cigarette in five months. "You can bank on that. I gave myself a goal of two years here. It took that long to lose myself. It'll take that long to find me."

His gaze swept the desolate landscape. "Well, you sure aren't going to find anything else here. I've come by to pick up the weekly order forms. How about running in with me to Flagstaff Saturday while I fill them? We can squeeze in dinner before we make the trip back."

"I thought the BIA filled the requests at Tuba City."

"We usually do. But every quarter the Western Navajo Agency purchases supplies not available in Tuba City—mostly office equipment, medical supplies for our public health clinic, things like that."

The suggestion sounded heavenly. She paused on the small slab of cement that was supposed to serve as her apartment's front porch. "Marshall, you'd have to backtrack fifty miles to pick me up."

"Cody often comes into Tuba City on Saturday. I'm sure I could persuade him to stop by your apartment."

She almost said no. But she would be damned if she was going to let the strained feelings between her and Cody spoil her chance for an outing. Then again, he might refuse Marshall's request. "I'd like that very much."

"Good, I'll give you a call tomorrow at the school office to let you know what time Cody'll pick you up."

"What?" she mocked. "Use the school's telephone for personal calls?"

He grinned. "It's an emergency."

Cody's frame cast a large shadow through the screen door.

"Let me get my purse," she told him. Why did she have to feel so self-conscious?

She grabbed her shoulder bag off the double bed and looked over her shoulder in the mirror. The white designer jeans didn't hug her rear too tightly. With the matching denim jacket, cerise satin blouse and strappy sandals, she looked casual enough to spend the day shopping in

Flagstaff's decidedly western shops and still chic enough for most of its restaurants. And to think the metropolis of Phoenix was only two hours further. It was enough to make her giddy.

Cody was already in the pickup. She climbed inside the cab, keeping to the far side. He spared her only the briefest of glances. She had become accustomed to that from the Navajo. In the school, at the trading post, moving among them, it was almost as if she didn't exist. Their eyes never made contact with hers. But she was sure that later at night, over the hogan fires, every detail of her appearance would be recounted, just as she was sure that Cody's sharp eyes missed nothing in their swift inventory, down to the pins that held her hair in its low knot. It was the first time in months that she had bothered to do anything with her hair but pull it back in a clasp at her nape.

"Escaping to the big city?" he asked and revved up the engine.

"No," she said tartly. "Only visiting." She slid a glance at him. He wore the usual boots and jeans, which rode low over his hips. A faded denim jacket had been added. The worn black Stetson slouched low over his eyes. "Are you? Escaping to the big city?"

He laughed, a low but pleasant sound that she liked. "Hardly. I feel like I'm bearding the lions in their den when I find myself anywhere with concrete pavement and steel buildings and blaring music and car horns. And people jammed elbow to elbow."

She sensed that he was alluding to his own fear, a right that he had reminded her even an adult had. It would seem that the two of them could carry on a normal discussion without getting into an argument after all. Maybe the fifty-two-mile trip to Tuba City wouldn't be as disagreeable as she had thought. "After living here, I can see how you would feel that way. The tranquility. The untouched beauty . . ."

"Oh, don't fool yourself, Mrs. Dennis. The tranquility and the untouched beauty are nice for a change. But soon the quiet begins to grate on the nerves, and the untouched beauty gets awful stark and empty-looking for people like you."

The attempt at a congenial conversation was sliding dangerously. "And just who are 'people like me'?" she asked, trying to keep the friction from her voice.

Momentarily he took his eyes off the dirt road that dipped and jumped ahead ad infinitum and shot her a cool glance that she could only interpret as contempt. "Patronizing women who come here to play the 'grand lady.' You come with your donations and your impersonal charity. You come with your electricity and technology, unwilling to live the simple life you claim you seek. You come with your Sunday religion for a people whose every daily action is directed toward the Great Spirit."

She bit back a furious retort, because she knew that a large part of what he had said was true. And she also sensed that he wanted to make her angry, that normally, with anyone else, he would have let the subject pass. Why was he so hostile toward her?

"I believe you have made your point, Mr. Strawhand," she said, keeping her face toward the open window, "but I'm not leaving Kaibeto." She was grateful for the wind in her face, cooling her. She would not lose her composure. Marshall had told her that she didn't belong at Kaibeto, Miss Halliburton didn't want her there and Cody had made it quite clear what he thought of her. And sometimes she herself wished she were anywhere else. But there *was* nowhere else. She was going to have to prove herself here.

Moments later Cody swung the pickup off the main dirt road onto one that was little more than wagon wheel ruts through the sage and broomgrass and low cactus. "Where are we going?" she asked, hiding the concern she felt.

Wasn't he part Indian? Hadn't she felt that primitive side of him? He had a sheer force that wasn't easily reckoned with. In this desolation he could easily dispose of her. Oh, come on, she told herself, you're being melodramatic.

"Just beyond Camel Rock—there"—he pointed to the jagged hunk of rock plopped in the midst of the empty desert—"is a hogan. A friend is going with us."

"Oh," she murmured, both relieved and ashamed at the direction her thoughts had erroneously taken.

Once the pickup passed Camel Mountain, the tail end of White Mesa with its "window" formation came into view. Cody braked the pickup to a

halt, but she couldn't immediately see anything
for the flurry of dust. When it settled, she spotted
the hogan. With its low and dim silhouette, it was
almost camouflaged by its natural habitat. As in
all Indian homes, its doorway, curtained by a
flour sack, faced east. A few yards away was a
miniature hogan, the bath house, and a brush
arbor that was in reality the summer hogan.

"Is something wrong?" she asked, when Cody
made no move to get out.

"It's courteous to wait a few minutes," he
explained. No hint of his earlier antagonism shaded his voice now. As if to reestablish the earlier
friendly atmosphere, he added, "Tradition warns
that evil spirits may be following guests, and these
tchindees must not be led in on friends."

When he opened the pickup's door, two
women stepped through the hogan's curtained
doorway. The older woman, who toted several
folded rugs, was dressed in the typical flounced
skirt, velveteen blouse and men's work boots.
The younger, contrastingly, wore jeans and a
pink tee shirt printed with the words *Navajo
Power*.

When the two got closer, Abbie could see that
the older woman had skin the texture of a wadded
paper sack. She wore her hair in the traditional
squash-blossom knot. Her blouse had silver quarters and dimes that served as buttons—for trading
at the post for purchases. With a start of surprise
Abbie recognized the younger woman.

"Hello, Dalah," she called out warmly, glad to
see a familiar face.

Dalah grinned and waved. Cody took the rugs from the old woman and tossed them in the back of the pickup. She murmured something to him and turned to leave, but Dalah walked with Cody around to Abbie's side of the pickup.

Cody opened the door and said, "You already know Dalah, Mrs. Dennis. She's going with us."

Abbie had no choice but to slide over to the center of the seat. A spring stuck up beneath the worn seatcovers, tilting her against Cody. Never had she felt more like a fifth wheel. And she also felt very old sitting next to the young, effervescent Dalah.

Dalah talked easily of subject after subject, starting with the rugs that were highly valued for their beauty and durability. "I'm taking them to Tuba City, where they bring a better price because of the tourist trade." Of the next sing she said, "It's going to be held at the Tribal Chapter House." An exhibit that she had read about in *Southwestern Art* also interested her. "Paul Speckled Rock will be showing his sculptures at Flagstaff's Anasazi Gallery of Art. You know, Mrs. Dennis, Cody's jewelry is on display there."

"How nice," Abbie said with a glance at Cody's noncommittal expression. A hard face, certainly an uncompromising one. But sometimes she unexpectedly caught a light of compassion in his eyes—with the boy Robert, later with Dalah's mother when he took the rugs. She couldn't help adding, "So even the Indian is disposed to crass, capitalistic commercialism."

He grinned amiably and laid his arm along the

back of the seat. "Oh, the Indians had been involved in commerce, Mrs. Dennis, even before they were persuaded to trade Manhattan for a couple of beaded necklaces."

"Touché," Abbie said, ceding that particular victory to him.

The rest of the ride into Tuba City was mixed with the radio's BIA Navajo program, indecipherable to her, and spurts of conversation between Dalah and Cody. From certain things that were said, Abbie gathered that he wasn't married.

She was acutely aware of Cody's arm above her shoulders, his thigh touching hers. Like an infatuated schoolgirl, she thought with self-disgust. She recalled her first date with Brad and the breathless wait to see if he would kiss her. Would Cody? Damn! She really must be going through a mid-life crisis!

Cody swung the pickup into the Western Navajo Agency's paved parking lot. As if he had been waiting for them, Marshall came out and crossed to the pickup with eager strides. He leaned on Dalah's open window. "Hi, Dalah." His welcoming smile lingered on Abbie. "Glad you could make it, Abbie. Thanks for bringing her, Cody."

"I wouldn't have missed the opportunity for the world."

Marshall seemed oblivious to the mockery in Cody's tone and went on to explain that Cody and Dalah had agreed to join them later for dinner. Abbie's vision of a pleasant evening rapidly faded. With the prospect of the meeting with Cody in her mind, the day lost some of its luster.

On the trip into Flagstaff she told Marshall about some of the pleasure and pain she found in teaching the Indian children. He listened, laughed and agreed with her observations, particularly about the need for firepit guards in the hogans.

"Marshall, the little ones who leave for the weekend often return with bad burns. Some are already scarred for life. Wendy Tso came back Sunday night with her palm badly blistered. Someone needs to convince the Indians that their hogans must have some kind of guards in front of the firepits."

"Try telling that to the Indian Tribal Council," he said gloomily. "There are some customs and superstitions that are difficult to break. The firepit is their stove, heater, ceremonial center. To alter its design"—he shook his head in a weary gesture —"it'd be like our trying to buck city hall."

The soaring San Francisco Peaks, sacred to the Navajo, and the increasing number of ponderosa pines and quaking aspens announced the proximity of Flagstaff. Fields of sunflowers banked either side of the superhighway. Despite its frontier charm the area boasted many modern industries.

While Marshall visited an office supply house in the new Flagstaff Mall, she desultorily shopped at some of its boutiques but found nothing she really wanted or could afford.

Somehow the fads and frills seemed frivolous to her now. After Marshall finished, they stopped off at the community hospital, where she requested a supply of medicated salve. Later they

shopped at an enormous modern supermarket.
They each pushed a cart and checked items off the
teachers' order forms.

"I never knew I could miss shopping so!" she
said, restraining the impulse to put a little of
everything into her cart.

Too soon, dinnertime approached. Marshall
chose Granny's Closet, a restaurant that resembled an old mining office. The interior was elabo-
rate, with a decor out of the twenties. Soft music
emanated from the lounge area, which was dim.
Abbie could make out college couples dancing
cheek to cheek. How often had she and Brad
done that? Three or four times in twenty years? It
seemed that instead of dancing there had always
been business deals to negotiate over after-dinner
drinks. Yet most of the time Brad had been
involved in what had seemed, to her, an unpro-
ductive life—golf, poker, tennis, cocktail parties.

On the far side of the dance floor, she saw
Dalah and Cody already seated on one of the
lounge's deep sofas, talking across two large
glasses of what appeared to be frozen margaritas.
Cody's arm was draped along the back of the sofa
behind Dalah's head. He said something to
Dalah, leaning close to make himself heard, and
she laughed merrily.

Marshall steered Abbie through the maze of
small tables. Despite all the noise, the muted
lights, the press of people, she knew exactly at
what point Cody became aware that she was in
the room, though she was sure he hadn't yet seen
her. The knowledge was like a jolt, stunning her.

Was there indeed something to the chemical attraction theory?

Self-consciously she acknowledged Dalah's happy greeting and Cody's nod. Unless she wanted to appear obviously rude—or, more likely, betray the unsettling effect he had on her—she would have to make eye contact with Cody at some point. She slid into the tufted barrel chair across from the low sofa. "How went your day?" she asked, forcing her gaze to meet his heavy-lidded one.

Beneath the bandana, his eyes seemed to study hers briefly; then his gaze dropped to her mouth. This she was used to by now, for the Navajos tended to watch the lips rather than the eyes when conversing. Still, she found his gaze on her mouth strangely disconcerting. "Profitable," he said.

"Yes," Dalah said with enthusiasm. "Not only were the rugs snapped up by the Indian Arts Center, but a representative of the Dallas Trade Center was there. He wants to take Cody's work on commission."

"Great!" Marshall said. "At this rate you'll never have to go back to roughnecking around the oil fields again."

Cody cocked a grin. "I still think about it when the checks are slow to arrive."

Marshall began talking about the closing of the reservation's coal mines, deferring to Cody for an opinion. Cody merely shrugged. "It's a catch-22. The tribal council could have placed more lenient conditions on the companies that came into the reservation to mine. Things like the mandatory employment of Navajos as superintendents, the guarantee that a percentage of the profit go back to the Navajo Nation, the reclamation of the land, are all hard for them to work with.

"But then," Cody added, "the United States government pays the Navajo anyway, so most of the men wonder why they should work at all. We're being emasculated, and it's as much our fault as the government's."

Cody turned the talk to a lighter subject, and the conversation flowed easily until Dalah excused herself to go to the ladies' room and Marshall left to check on their dinner reservations. Abbie was left alone with Cody. She pretended interest in the couples on the dance floor. Why hadn't she thought of going to the ladies' room with Dalah? she asked herself.

She nearly jumped when Cody rose. "Let's dance, Abbie," he said quietly.

It was the first time that he had used her given name, and the way he said it—it was like he had actually reached out and touched her. She forced herself to look up calmly into his dark face. "All right."

The tune was an old one, and she went into his arms with racing emotions that she tried to rein in. She looked anywhere but up into his eyes. Other women eyed Cody surreptitiously. Undoubtedly he was handsome in a rugged way. He carried himself with a proud grace and exuded an animal magnetism. Despite his Indian appearance, he fit easily into the disco scene along with the cowboys, college students and stocky lumberjacks present in the room. She offered no resistance when his encircling arm at her waist firmly pulled her closer to him.

Cody had wanted to hold her against him ever since he met her. He held her now, his hand lowering to firmly press her hips against his, so that his body was keenly attuned to her feminine contours. Had he foolishly thought that by merely holding her he would lose interest? Was it her icy reserve that challenged him? She acted like some damn royal princess. Yet there had been other women in his life . . . beautiful, elegant, poised.

But it was more than that. She had a presence that couldn't be bought with money or absorbed from her environment. Her voice was soft and low with a gentle assurance and without the strident tones of some women.

He had noted her ring finger, encircled by a simple gold wedding band. Why was she separated from her husband—and did she love the man? He told himself that she was running, that soon she would run back, that he did not intend to be part of her catharsis while she was there.

He pulled her tightly to him, as if by causing her pain he could shatter her self-containment. Her breasts flattened against his chest. He wished he could bury himself in her. She tilted her head back to look at him, her lips softly parted, her eyes reflecting her confusion. "I have other plans tonight," he said harshly. "Marshall will have to take you back to Kaibeto."

"He was going to anyway," she snapped and walked off the dance floor to join Dalah and Marshall, who were engrossed in conversation.

Rude. Detestable. Arrogant. Then why the magic? That was the only way Abbie could think to describe that moment when Cody had held her. What had happened to her practicality, her logic, her analytical reasoning?

The rest of the evening—the interminable dinner, the long drive back to Kaibeto with Marshall, the storing of the groceries in the cafeteria for distribution later—all seemed a blur, even the moment when Marshall parked the car in front of her apartment and took her in his arms. She had responded with a light kiss, her first kiss in more than twenty years from any man other than her husband. And she had felt nothing. He hadn't pressed her for more, simply left with a promise to come by soon.

Monday morning before class she toted the cardboard box of aspirin, salve and other medicines that she had obtained from the hospital over to the children's dormitory. She knew that Dalah had the Sunday morning shift off. Had she spent the night with Cody?

Really, she must put the odious man from her mind. She wanted no more entanglements to complicate the life she was making for herself.

She found Dalah going down a line of little girls, lifting their skirts. The Indian girl looked up at Abbie and grinned. "Panty check," she explained. "Our more traditional women don't wear underwear beneath their long skirts, so we have to retrain their daughters."

Laughing, Abbie held out the box she carried. "I've brought more supplies—soap, shampoo and other items."

She was about to leave when Dalah forestalled her with a copy of *Southwestern Art*. "It's the article I was telling you about—about Cody," the Indian girl said proudly. "I thought maybe you would like to read it."

During the morning break Abbie glanced over the three-column article, feeling strangely dissatisfied. The author had written about Cody's technique at silversmithing, the purity of the designs that were untouched by foreign influence, the following he was gathering in the art world, but little about the man himself. There wasn't even a photo. She sensed that that was Cody's doing, that he would resent an invasion of his privacy.

She slapped the magazine closed. So much for her charge about Cody Strawhand trying to pass himself off as a craftsman. He really was a master craftsman of some repute.

Reading about him was no way to start off the day, and things got no better. It started sprinkling, which made the walk to the cafeteria at lunch a dampening experience. "They could have laid out the grounds better," Becky grumbled.

The girl seemed to take out her disgruntlement on the children. When Joey Kills the Soldier hesitated with his tray before the side dishes, unable to pronounce the one he wanted, she snapped, "Macaroni—say it, macaroni!"

The small boy's eyes, as large and dark as a fawn's, welled up. His lower lip trembled, but he didn't cry. Becky grabbed his shoulder and shook him. "Say it, Joey. Ma-ca-ron-i."

"Becky!"

At Abbie's reproving snap the entire cafeteria quieted. The Indian women behind the counter stopped their work; the children's spoons paused; the teachers already eating craned their heads to see what the disturbance was.

The young teacher glanced defiantly at Abbie. "That's the only way these Indian children will ever learn! You can't keep babying them, Mrs. Dennis."

"But you don't need to humiliate them, either. Now, release him."

A long moment passed, then the younger woman pushed the boy from her. "You'll find out I'm right," she told Abbie and walked away with her tray.

The cafeteria noise resumed. Abbie bent down and put her arm around the little boy. "It's all right, Joey." Did he understand her? And would it ever be all right? How did one explain to a child that his mother was in a West Virginia prison for women and that she wasn't sure who his father was? Sometimes Abbie thought her concern for the children and their backgrounds made her job that much worse.

"Give Joey a bowl of macaroni," she told the woman behind the counter.

When classes resumed, Abbie discovered that Robert Tsinnijinnie hadn't returned from the cafeteria with the other children. She was obviously going to reach a new low in an already hellish day. Miss Halliburton had probably heard by now about the episode in the cafeteria with Becky and was no doubt already foaming at the mouth. It wouldn't help Abbie's record if the principal found out that her student had run off again.

Abbie knew where the boy was. She would just have to bite the bullet and go after him. A steady but light drizzle accompanied her as she made her way toward the bridge. She darted an uneasy glance over the railing. Puddles dotted the wash far below. Keeping her eyes straight ahead, she clutched the slick railing and hurried across. She kept to the wash's edge, where the ground was smoother, but didn't dare let herself look down again.

The once natty tux-shirt with its black grosgrain ribbon at the neck clung damply to her chilled skin, and the crisp black A-line skirt hung in limp folds about her thighs. She wondered if her effort was worth it. Robert would only continue to run away. Psychologists said that when a child got to be his age it was too late to change his psychological makeup. Still, if she wanted to keep her record unblemished, she had to find the boy. And she didn't even like him.

At the same time that she sighted the mission's adobe walls through the mist of rain, she heard Cody's shout from the doorway. Startled, she halted in her tracks as he came loping down the incline toward her. When he drew close enough,

she could see the anger that darkened his face.
"You stupid idiot!" he shouted. His hand grabbed
her wrist.

He spun and yanked her along behind him.
Caught off balance, she slipped, falling face first
in the mud. He didn't halt but dragged her behind
him. Twice she struggled to her feet only to trip
again. When they reached the door, he released
her wrist. Wearily she sank to her knees, her
blouse hanging half open, her muscles trembling.

"Get up."

"Leave me alone," she gasped. Her gaze rested
dully on the mud-splattered boots of the man
before her.

He hunkered down next to her. His hand
grasped her chin and jerked it toward the wash.
"Look."

She tried to focus her gaze on whatever it was
he wanted her to see. Then she saw it. And heard
it. The great white wall of water that roared down
the wash, obliterating the old banks, creating new
ones. "Flash flood," he grated by her ear.

She watched, fascinated. Behind it rode up-
rooted trees, an overturned automobile that bobbled like a top, the floating carcass of a cow. She
shivered uncontrollably and looked up into
Cody's granite face. She was so close that she
could make out the green flecks that speckled the
brown irises of his narrowed eyes. "I could have
been killed," she breathed.

The violence of the moment surrounded them.
The rain thundered down on the mud-sluiced
ground. Lightning crackled, slicing through the

black sky. Nature's wrath seemed to communicate itself to Cody. His fingers dug painfully into Abbie's arms, and he caught her up against him. His mouth ground down on hers in a brutal kiss. She didn't care. The same violence that coursed through him, claimed her. She answered his kiss, wrapping her arms about his shoulders. She opened her mouth to his, savoring its warmth and trembling at the savagery of his tongue.

With a need that was as old as mankind but that was new to her, she clung to him. She half moaned with frustration that her sitting position prevented her from knowing the feeling of his entire length pressed against hers. Suddenly Cody withdrew, setting her from him. As if she were dazed, her eyes opened slowly. At her bewildered look, he nodded slightly to his left. Her gaze followed the direction of his nod. Robert stood in the far doorway. His shuttered eyes watched them.

Her arms slid down from Cody's shoulders. She attempted to stand, bracing herself against the doorjamb. While Cody crossed the room, saying something in the Navajo tongue that seemed to her only a series of intonations, she tried to close her gaping blouse with numb fingers that didn't seem to want to obey her brain's signals.

Cody came back to stand before her. She looked up at him, trying to read what was in his eyes. They were as impassive as Robert's had been. At last he removed her clammy fingers from the buttons and fastened them himself. "You're chilled," he said flatly. "I'll fix coffee while you dry off; then I'll take you and Robert back to the school.''

The bathroom was about the size of a monk's cubicle, with modern plumbing added. Man's shower, no tub. Terra cotta tiles and adobe walls. Above the azulejo counter was an octagon mirror set in a hand-carved wooden frame. Abbie saw the pale face that looked back at her, the tawny blond hair that straggled about her shoulders, the glazed blue eyes. She blinked several times, trying to orient herself. Shock, she knew, often made people react strangely.

The Red Cross classes given by the Junior Service League had outlined a victim's reactions after a catastrophe: first, the disorientation; then, after the shock wore off, the individual's actions were dominated by suggestibility; extreme gratitude followed.

Yes, she decided, stepping out of her skirt and slip, that was what it was. The shock of the flash flood, her relief at being alive—she slid out of her blouse and picked up the towel that Cody had left—those accounted for what had happened, the way she had clung to him and kissed him. Sheer gratitude. Briskly she toweled her hair. She had nothing to be ashamed of. Anyone could have forgotten herself following a moment of crisis like that.

The door opened, and she half turned. Cody stood there. She should have shielded herself, but she couldn't have moved had her life depended on it. In that fraction of a moment his gaze swept over her, missing nothing, not the slender shape of her legs nor the faint marks that stretched across her abdomen, not the full milk-white breasts penciled with pale blue veins nor the eyes that glittered like polished turquoise. His own eyes smoldered like a fire's banked embers. Flashes of heat crackled through her.

"Your coffee is ready. And here are some dry clothes." The door closed behind him.

Expecting to crumple any second, she leaned over the chrome and ceramic sink and drew in several deep breaths. What was wrong with her?

The blue-plaid flannel shirt, much too large for her, she knotted at her waist; the leather breech cloth hung past her thighs. She couldn't believe it, a loincloth!

"It was the only thing I thought would fit," Cody remarked laconically when she stepped into the kitchen and sheepishly waved her hand at the brief garment that covered her lower torso. He set the cup of aromatic coffee down on the wrought iron and glass table. On the walls were hung copper utensils and clay pots and ollas.

Carefully she slid into the chair. Why all the caution, Abbie Dennis, when you've displayed every intimate part of your body for him? Almost, she mentally corrected with a furious blush. "You really wear this—this loincloth?" she asked, sipping at the steaming coffee with affected nonchalance.

"I have." With his own cup in hand he took a seat at the opposite end of the table. He wore no headband, and his damp collar-length hair swung with the movement. "When I've been called upon for a sing."

"A sing?"

"Most Navajo sings are a combination of religious ceremony, social event and festivity." He smiled. "But at all of them a patient must be present."

He should smile more often, she thought. Her hand on the cup loosened its tense grip. There was no reason why the two of them couldn't carry on a civilized conversation. "Where's Robert?"

He swallowed some coffee. "At the forge. He's learning to make a bracelet. He wants to give it to his father when he comes for Robert at the Christmas holidays."

She looked down into her half-empty cup. "I hope his father does come. Some of the parents come every weekend. Sometimes the fathers sit on the steps for half a day, waiting for school to end. One of the mothers never fails to bring a candy bar and a can of soda from the trading post. Her daughter knows exactly when she comes over the hill by the color of her skirt. Other parents . . ." She shrugged, not trusting her voice.

"Other parents," he finished for her in a harsh voice, "like Robert's, will never come, because there's no way they can raise the money."

In that moment she felt allied with Cody as she identified with the hopelessness of the Indians' situation, a sense of oneness that she had never felt with the teachers. Dorothy cared, but her mind was more on retirement than the problems that Abbie occasionally broached. And Becky— she thought only of her dates with her lumberjack and couldn't have cared less about the children. Linda was involved with her toddler. Maybe, Abbie thought, I would do better to emulate the other teachers . . . to do my best at teaching but never let myself get involved. That's why I'm in this mess now . . . foolishly sitting here in a loin-cloth, no less.

She looked up to find Cody silently observing her. What was he thinking? She wished she had a cigarette. Why hadn't she bought a supply in Flagstaff to stash away for the stress times? Like now? "At dinner the other night—in Flagstaff— Marshall mentioned something about you rough-necking. Did you work on any of the Navajo oil rigs?"

He finished his coffee. "No. After college I headed down to South America and found work in the oil fields there."

She wanted to ask why there, in South America. But the conversation was beginning to border on the personal, and the last thing she wanted was to get involved on a personal level with anyone, and especially not this man who alerted all her senses to some unnamed danger.

She played it safe and selected an innocuous subject. "Where did you attend college?"

He reached behind himself for a cigarette package on the counter and shook one out. "Arizona State University." The match's flare briefly lit his dark eyes, and smoke spiraled up between them.

This was getting nowhere at all. "You have a unique home," she said nervously.

"My home, the Navajos' land."

"You sound like some motion picture Indian!" she bit out.

"Because I don't waste time talking when there's something else I'd rather be doing?"

"I don't know what you're talking about."

He eyed her steadily. "Don't you? Then why are you here?"

She pushed herself away from the table. "To get Robert, what do you think? And it's your fault I'm such a mess. If I hadn't been trying to keep to the bank of the wash like you told—"

He shoved the chair back and rose. She flinched, her nerves seeming to be strung as tightly as the strings of a tennis racket. Her breath came in ragged wisps. "I think I better go back."

He resumed his wooden Indian expression. "All right. I'll go for Robert while you get your clothes."

Chapter 4

"SHIRT."

Abbie held up Cody's shirt, which, after more than two weeks, she still hadn't had the courage to return. "Put your lips like this"—she puckered her lips—"and blow softly. Shhhh. Shirt."

The children's voices, all but Robert's, said the word in unison. He steadfastly stared out the window. She knew that he was very much aware of her frustration with his refusal to speak. His black eyes couldn't hide the perverse pleasure he took in thwarting her. *You'll say shirt yet, you little savage.* She half considered passing him on to the second grade whether he merited it or not. At least he hadn't spit at her again.

"Good!" She praised the other children's effort at the English word.

The need for the Indian children to learn the primary English words that Anglo children their age already knew slowed down her progress in teaching the basics of reading. She spent the rest of the morning working with the consonants. When the bell rang, she stopped Robert as he filed past. The boy looked at her obliquely, as though awaiting some reprimand. She handed him the shirt and loincloth.

"The next time you see your friend Cody," she said slowly and distinctly, "would you give these to him?"

Not a flutter of an eyelash. Did he understand her? At last he inclined his head in the barest of nods. He understood her; he understood that she knew he would run away again sometime. A sparkle of bared teeth showed between his lips. She would have called it a victory smile. But it was her victory, too. She had communicated with him, at least.

It was going to be a good day, she was sure. The day got even better when at recess Becky stopped her at the crosswalk to apologize. "I'm sorta sorry about what happened a couple of weeks back." The young teacher toyed with an oily strand of hair and looked off toward Navajo Mountain as if it were of captivating interest. "I guess I'm just getting cabin fever. You know, it kinda gets to you after a while—living way out here in the middle of nowhere."

Abbie found herself also looking out toward the great mauve dome. "Yes, I know," she murmured in agreement. She must forget the Navajo.

He wasn't even Navajo, she reminded herself disagreeably. And he wasn't some medicine man, some shaman who could control her thoughts and actions. No man would ever have that hold on her again. She would do *what* she wanted, *when* she wanted. She simply needed to be with people who were at least semisophisticated more often. Why hadn't Marshall dropped by to see her?

The day seemed to take a sour turn and stayed that way when Delbert Yellowman later closed the classroom door on Julie Begay's hand. The only sound the girl made was a sharp intake of breath. No whimpering, no tears. Navajo children rarely cried. But the fingers were swelling so rapidly that it was difficult for Abbie to distinguish the knuckles.

She left Linda McNabb, who was on break, in charge of the class and, with Julie in tow, hurried over to her apartment. Thank goodness she hadn't prepared her can of frozen orange juice yet! She grabbed the can from the freezer and quickly bound it to Julie's palm with a dish towel.

The hand would need to be X-rayed. "Let's go," she told the six-year-old, who uttered not a word of protest.

Miss Halliburton did. Her face seemed to turn the same shade of blue gray as her wig. "This is your fault, Mrs. Dennis," she said coldly. "You are supposed to be supervising these children."

Abbie faced the martinet across the office desk. "It was an accident, Miss Halliburton. Accidents do happen."

"A teacher who cannot properly watch the children is not fit to teach!"

Never had Abbie felt so frustrated. She didn't know whether to cry or yell. "The child's hand needs proper medical treatment. May I take her to the public health clinic in Tuba City?"

"If you think you can get there without another accident. And the time you're absent—that time will have to be made up, you understand?"

"Time is no problem, Miss Halliburton. I have nothing but time."

Fuming, Abbie left the office with Julie silently trailing behind and crossed to the shed where the Jeep and wagon were kept side by side. The modern and the primitive. When she remembered that the Jeep was a stick shift, she thought she would cry for sure. All right, she told herself, you figured out the gears on Justin and Jason's motorcycles. The Jeep can't be too much different.

It was. She drove out of the school compound in reverse before she backed into a fence post. Julie laughed until tears were streaming down her rosy cheeks. This time Abbie did cry. She put her head in her hands and, leaning against the steering wheel, silently wept. Wept for twenty years of illusions and shattered dreams.

At last she lifted her head. The little girl's big black eyes watched her warily. Abbie laughed. "I'm just a foolish old woman, Julie Begay."

She tried the Jeep again. Finally she found first gear. The jungle green Jeep coughed and spurted and died when she pushed the stick shift into second. An infinite number of tries and five miles further down the road she mastered the movements from first to third gear. Fourth gear she gave up on.

It was Julie's first ride in a car, and the child's black eyes sparkled with delight during the fifty-mile trip. But the trip couldn't end soon enough for Abbie. When she pulled up into the BIA parking lot, she forgot to use the clutch, and the Jeep screeched to a whiplash-inducing halt and sputtered its last.

Marshall came around from behind his desk when she entered with Julie. He took one look at the dish towel wrapped hand and, without asking for any explanations, said, "I'll run you over to the public health offices."

"I thought they were in the same building," Abbie groaned, but she let him usher her and Julie back through the door. He began laughing, and she saw that he was looking at the preposterous angle at which she had parked the Jeep. "It was the best I could do."

"And you did it wonderfully, my girl!" He put his arm around her shoulder and squeezed it. "Now," he said to Julie, "let's take care of that hand."

While the young doctor on duty X-rayed Julie's hand, Abbie gave the receptionist the little information she knew about the girl. When the receptionist paused at "father's occupation," Abbie had to smile. If asked, all children gave their father's occupation as tribal policeman. The job carried the most prestige. "Tribal policeman," Abbie replied.

In fact, Julie's father had been a coal miner. But since the reservation mines had been shut down the year before, he was among the many who sat listlessly in front of his hogan. With the money from the Bureau of Indian Affairs and the uranium royalty checks from the Navajo Nation, the men simply had no incentive to work. They had been hunters. Now food and shelter were provided for their families.

Marshall flashed her a conspiratorial smile.

"I needed that smile," she told him while they sat waiting on a vinyl-covered couch that had holes like a sieve. "And a cigarette—but don't tempt me."

"It's been that bad a morning, eh?"

"The BIA's stringent rules about emergencies —they're so damned frustrating, Marshall."

"You can imagine how the public health doctor feels when a child is brought in with trachoma or a mother with TB and he has to say, 'Sorry, but we don't have the money to send you to Phoenix.'"

The hopelessness again. . . .

The doctor came back with Julie. "Two fingers broken. I've splinted them, and they should be all right in four or five weeks." He smiled at Abbie. "Your ice pack was quick thinking, Mrs. Dennis."

She laughed. "Brownie first aid, doctor."

"Were you really a Brownie?" Marshall asked later after he had helped Julie into the Jeep and come around to Abbie's side.

"You bet."

He braced his hands on the open window. "I can just picture you—knobby knees and pigtails."

"How did you guess?"

He grinned. "That's the kind that always grows into a beautiful, warm, intelligent woman."

She started the engine. "Marshall, come by for coffee sometime when you're at Kaibeto."

He winked. "I've been waiting for the invitation."

A haze of smoke permeated the Phoenix hotel bar. In the corner of the booth Cody propped his arm on one raised knee and watched the woman sitting next to him. She was nothing at all like Abbie Dennis. Shorter, with russet brown hair. Green eyes instead of blue. Too much makeup. Yet she had that same indefinable air of sophistication. But not quality, he thought, recalling Orville's story about the orange juice can and Julie Begay's broken fingers.

The woman—what was her name? Jacqueline? —leaned toward him, her overblown breasts swaying enticingly beneath the expensive dress of red taffeta, as she had meant them to. Her beringed fingers played with his horsehead belt buckle. "Is it true you won this riding bulls?"

"Saddle broncs."

"Marvin says you were a world champion."

"National intercollegiate champion. It helped pay my way through college."

"Marvin says—"

"Where *is* Marvin?"

The Scottsdale dealer's wife looked up at him innocently through thickly applied mascara. "I thought I told you. He isn't going to join us until seven."

Marvin Klein, famous for the prestigious list of merchants he bought jewelry from, had been asking Cody for more than a year to let him handle Cody's work. But it had been Abbie's perceptive thrust—that he was hiding out from society—which had made him accept Klein's wheedling to come to Phoenix to discuss a possible consignment.

The consignment would mean an international market for his jewelry, something he had always rebeled against. He felt only revulsion for people who valued a piece of jewelry for its ostentatious price rather than its beauty. And he had learned early—at his mother's knee, he thought with bitterness—that the women who moved in the upper echelons of society made that kind of judgment as a matter of course.

Jacqueline's finger slipped over the belt buckle to rub against his stomach muscles like a purring cat rubbing against a leg. "Actually, darling, I do all the primary negotiations for Marvin. Ever since I saw the pair of earrings you did for the wife of the president of the Philippines, I've been after Marvin to snap you up."

Cody's gaze burned through the smoky haze. "Oh? You've been a guest of the Filipino first family?"

Her finger burrowed between the buttons of his

shirt. "Well, no. It was a photo in the paper—one of the president visiting your shop—that first caught my attention."

Cody had limited his clientele to a select few. His royalties on the South American oil well investments he had made enabled him to sell his work as he chose.

But perhaps Abbie's infuriating observation was right; perhaps it was more than just artistic temperament that influenced his sequestered lifestyle. In the rare moments when he was tempted to philosophize, usually after one drink too many, he often wondered if he had rejected the accouterments of celebrity to avoid the possibility that society could reject him.

Damn Abbie Dennis and her perceptiveness. Whether he wanted to admit it or not, she had an elusive quality, a refinement honed by the years, that he had found in no other woman. No, that wasn't completely true. His stepmother possessed it, and she was full-blooded Indian.

He tried to remind himself that Abbie was married, but so was the very attractive woman across from him; he tried to remind himself that his world could offer Abbie nothing, nor hers him; but then, Jacqueline Klein could offer him nothing, either. She wanted only to take. At that moment—as she had for a long time—she wanted him.

"Marvin says you are a master artist," Jacqueline said now, her fingers dropping lower. "I bet you're also a master lover."

He tossed off his scotch and soda, set the glass down and removed her hand. "Tell Marvin to call me when he's ready to negotiate."

Jacqueline's gasp of indignation was lost on him as he rose and made his way out of the bar. Her sensuous body would not appease the hunger he felt, a hunger more of the soul than the senses.

His thoughts turned once more to Abbie, the afternoon of the flash flood and that one glimpse of her lovely, exquisite body. He wanted to run one fingertip along the marks that feathered across her stomach. She had been a mother. How many times? And she was still a wife. He wanted to know more about her, the mother and the wife. Abbie the woman . . . he was falling in love with her. A taboo. Different cultures, different race. Though he was more white than Indian, he thought like an Indian. They couldn't possibly blend as one. Perhaps that was why he had tried to frighten her that afternoon of the flash flood with his angry words of wanting her.

His words . . . all empty threats. And his thoughts . . . all dangerous.

In the soft light of dusk the wind-blown patterns in the red sand contrasted with the jagged lava rocks and cinder stone strewn across the area by the violent volcanic activity of thousands of years ago. The land was different from Pennsylvania's soft, rolling hills, and the maple and walnut trees that autumn had already colored with reds and yellows and oranges.

And the people were different. There existed in the Indians none of that frantic need to do everything, to experience everything, exhibited by the Anglos. At times Abbie was frustrated by the slower pace, but most of the time she simply felt like the outsider she was, a foreigner.

Perhaps that was what prompted her to accept Dalah's invitation to have dinner with the young woman's family. Such invitations were not normally issued to a non-Indian. The Navajo were a shy but proud people. Yet Abbie had established a friendship with Dalah—essentially because she often visited the children's dormitory in the evenings and helped Dalah, though that wasn't part of her duties. Then, too, Dalah sensed that Abbie was genuinely interested in the Navajo language and customs, which helped bridge the distance created by their cultural differences.

Though the autumn days were radiant with sun, the evenings were chilly, and Abbie missed the warmth offered by a car. She rode on the buckboard seat of the wagon with Dalah and her bearlike father, who wore his long hair in the old way, with wool yarn wrapping the still blue-black strands into the squash-blossom style. But his clothes were modern western wear—jeans, plaid shirt, battered felt hat and soiled sheepskin jacket.

He held the reins loosely in his weather-gnarled hands and Dalah teased him about the plodding horse. "Whenever I suggest getting a car, my father always reminds me that hay is cheaper than gas."

"And Sunflower is more reliable than the school's burros," Abbie added.

Dalah laughed and related her father's joke on a *bil'langali'*, a tourist, who had come by their house. "The man stopped at our hogan yesterday and wanted to know what the smaller hogan was for. My father told him our bathhouse was a doghouse. The Anglo went away shaking his head in puzzlement."

Her father grinned broadly, as if he understood the English translation. Charmed by the man's delightful sense of humor, Abbie was beginning to feel more at ease . . . until Dalah said, "My family has also invited Cody, but he said he would have to come late."

Very late, Abbie hoped.

The hogan was crouched in a straggly grove of cedars. A rusted barrel, used as a child's bucking horse, was suspended by a rope from one of the sturdier trees. Not far away a pig rooted in the sunbaked earth. The hogan was not the typical earthen one that Abbie was accustomed to seeing but was constructed of cement and tarpaper. Inside, on the floor near the walls, were rolled sheepskins to be used later for sleeping. Abbie noted that the dirt floor had been watered and walked down. It looked as hygenically clean as any hospital. Yet it was difficult to imagine Dalah, who had been educated at Innermountain High School in Brigham City, living in what many would have considered substandard conditions.

Grateful for the warmth of the fire, she remembered to keep to the left of the firepit that burned with the nutlike scent of piñon. In a large pot over the fire something savory bubbled. An older woman, whom she recognized as Dalah's mother, rose and nodded. This time, instead of men's old work boots, Dalah's mother wore moccasins, with the five-inch strip of cotton wrapping up the leg to serve as a protection against cactus and snow.

A mewling cry drew Abbie's attention to the cradleboard not far from the woman. The cradleboard was made of cedar bark with, surprisingly, a Styrofoam mattress. "My brother, Victor," Dalah said. The child, of course, had another name—a private name that was never to be used.

Abbie knelt before Victor and playfully tickled his fat little chin with her forefinger. Like all Navajo babies, he was red with black eyes and lots of black hair. A turquoise nugget was suspended from the cradleboard's bow for good luck.

Three more children—two boys and a girl—materialized in the fire's light, and Abbie thought with rueful humor why Dalah's mother looked so old.

Without seeming to move her lips, the woman uttered something in the guttural Navajo tongue and Dalah said, "More water is needed. Would you like to come with me to the well?"

The well, drilled by the federal government, turned out to be a huge galvanized tank at the foot of an old wooden windmill. A few sheep grazed nearby. The number of sheep and cattle owned by a Navajo family was determined by their supply of juniper, pinion and greasewood.

As they carried the water in a bucket back to the hogan Abbie realized that she was reaching the most basic level of living. The water sloshed on her white denim jeans and jacket and on the smart leather boots where the dust collected in muddy lumps. Her arms ached, though the well was less than half a mile from the hogan. Dalah seemed not to notice the weight of the water bucket she toted.

Abbie almost dropped the bucket when she saw the pickup parked before the hogan. Her heart thudding, she followed Dalah inside. The girl's mother was pounding purple corn with a stone *mana* and a *metate*, and her father squatted on the far side of the firepit, deep in conversation with Cody. As always, Cody wore a mixture of Anglo and Indian clothing: faded jeans and a blue chambray shirt; a red flannel headband and high-top moccasins.

He didn't once glance in the women's direction, nor did Dalah make any effort to greet him. The two men talked to each other or sometimes to one of the children, but they ignored Abbie, Dalah and her mother. Abbie was not accustomed to indifference, and she found it difficult to sit quietly with Dalah and watch the mother fry sweet bread in deep mutton fat. Occasionally Dalah would chatter about something, but all of Abbie's senses were more attuned to the tall, good-looking man who sat behind her.

"You can't imagine how disappointed my mother was that I did not learn how to weave at the white man's school," Dalah was saying, and

Abbie forced herself to listen to the young Indian woman's soft voice speaking English rather than Cody's deep resonant voice speaking Navajo. When he made love to a woman, did he use Navajo endearments?

She shook off the intimate thought and refocused her attention on Dalah, who had moved further back into the hogan to show her the loom her mother used to weave the sheep's wool. "My mother designed her rug from linoleum floor sample," Dalah said, reverting to the Navajo's habit of not pluralizing words.

But Abbie heard only what went on behind her. Cody shifted his hunkered-down position, and she knew instinctively that he was watching her. Yet when she turned around he was lighting a cigarette.

Soon the family gathered around the firepit for dinner. Cody sat across from Abbie; Dalah and her mother were on either side of her. Tentatively she tasted the beans and stew. Across the fire she saw the mockery that curved Cody's lips. He said something in Navajo to Dalah, and the young woman laughed. "Cody reminds me to tell you that the stew is made of mutton."

"It does ease my qualms," Abbie said dryly. She had no reservations about the sweet bread. The air bubbles in it were filled with honey, and she thought she had never tasted anything so good.

Between bites the conversation was carried on in Navajo, with the children, all sharing Dalah's lovely dark eyes and rose-shaded cheeks, piping in like magpies. Not once did Cody accord Abbie the courtesy of addressing her, and she would have felt left out had it not been for Dalah, who translated much of the conversation into English —except for the final sentence Cody directed to her father before he uncrossed his moccasined feet to rise in one smooth motion.

"I have told Dalah's father I will save him the necessity of taking you back to the school," he translated himself as he spoke to her for the first time.

Abbie sat dumbfounded. To argue would have been discourteous to the older man. But she certainly did not want to return with Cody. This was the second time that she had been forced to accept his offer of transportation—and the last, she silently swore as she took his outstretched hand and let him pull her to her feet.

She thanked Dalah, whose face had a curious expression, and the girl's mother and father, who merely nodded. Cody shrugged into his denim jacket but didn't bother to help her with her own. Wordlessly he escorted her to his pickup, his hand firmly at her elbow, as if he thought she would bolt. She refused to say anything, either. She sat in furious silence as the vehicle picked its way down the rutted trail, lit by the headlights and the bright, frosted light of a pumpkin moon.

Cody shook a cigarette from its package and offered her one. She badly wanted and needed it. "No, thank you," she said stiffly, even so.

He pocketed the package and said, "Tonight you discovered what a narrow little world you lived in before coming to Kaibeto, didn't you?"

"Is that why you didn't once speak to me?" she asked in a voice tight with growing anger.

The lighter flared in the darkness of the cab, and he bent his dark head to the flame. "I didn't think you would notice."

She ignored his sarcasm. "You were unspeakably rude."

"Was I?" He returned his attention to the demands of the almost nonexistent road. "How many times has the white man done the same?"

"That's unfair!" she accused. "You're generalizing." She leaned toward him. Her voice was low and harsh, her clipped words rapid. "You were purposefully rude because you wanted to make me feel uncomfortable. You still want to prove that I don't belong at Kaibeto." She paused and caught her breath, then said in a puzzled tone, "You don't want me here, do you?"

Without taking the cigarette from between his lips, he muttered, "No."

"Why?"

He braked the pickup in the shadows of Camel Rock and flicked the half-smoked cigarette out the window. Looking straight ahead, he said, "Your kind—"

"I'm tired of you throwing 'my kind' up to me," she lashed out.

He swung to face her. "I've met others like you," he grated.

"But I'm not them!"

"I know."

It was said in such a muffled voice that she wasn't sure she had heard him. His hands shot out to grab her upper arms and jerk her against him. She should have pulled away, but something in the dark liquid eyes held her in an almost catatonic stupor, so that it seemed she ceased to breathe as he lowered his head to hers. His lips were hard with his anger, stunning her own lips to the point that she sat nearly passive beneath the onslaught of the kiss—until his lips softened almost imperceptibly and he matched his mouth to hers. Slowly she came alive to the sweet passion his kiss infused in her. Her hands, splayed defensively against his chest, slipped up in hesitant increments to clasp the muscled ridges of his shoulders.

The kiss after the flash flood—she had experienced its virulence and reveled in it. But this tenderness—it nearly undid her. Small tremors in her stomach rippled outward until her entire body was shaking.

"Open your mouth, Abbie," Cody mumbled in a husky voice against her trembling lips. Unwilling to think clearly, incapable of refusing, she did as he bade. His tongue played lightly on her bottom lip before shafting between the two of them to find her tongue.

The hands that had clasped his shoulders now clenched with unfamiliar feelings, feelings long forgotten, that coursed through her. Her tongue answered the primeval question his own posed. The kiss lasted a lifetime. . . . It lasted through the twenty years of homogenized love-making she had known. Its intensity staggered her. Inexplicably she wanted to cry, but the rising passion, setting her afire, quenched the need to release her emotions in tears and re-placed it with a stronger need, the invincible desire of one soul, one body, to fuse with an-other.

His lips relinquished hers to find the hollow of her throat. "Your mouth . . ." he said. "It tastes of the honey you ate tonight. I want to know how the rest of you tastes."

She murmured no protest when he pressed her down on the seat, his massive body half covering hers. His hand slid inside her jacket and under her cashmere sweater to rub tantalizingly along the curvature of her ribs. "Abbie," he muttered rhetorically, his lips feathering along her arched neck, "why did you have to come to Kaibeto?" His hand cupped the underswell of one breast. "Why couldn't you have stayed in your own safe little world?"

She didn't care what he was asking; she only wanted him to continue what he was doing to her. Again and again he kissed her so that mere thinking was impossible. His hand slipped lower to clamp about her hipbone and press into the concavity of her abdomen. Her hips shifted, arched to meet the gentle but persistent persua-sion of that hand. It slid under her sweater again and around to the small of her back to press her into him.

His lips found her ear to trace its delicate convolutions. He raised his head. His eyes glittered against the darkness. "Abbie, I want to make love to you."

"Love?" she echoed blankly. "I don't remember what it is." She shook her head, as if trying to clear away the fog of sensual lethargy that stupefied her brain. Her hands strained at his corded upper arms. "I know that you haven't one particle of affection for me, Cody, that you despise me . . . and still I want you."

He pulled away to sit up. "You're harmfully honest."

She laughed brightly, almost too spontaneously. "If I were, I wouldn't have fooled myself, even for a minute, about what was happening just now."

To her astonishment he pulled her upright and drew her jacket about her. "And what did happen?" he asked quietly as his nimble fingers prodded at the jacket's buttons.

"Nothing," she murmured after a moment.

"Exactly," he said coldly, precisely. "But it could have."

She flared at his words, but he ignored her furious sputter. Finished with the buttons, he started the pickup. "As I told you before, Abbie, your kind doesn't belong out here. You belong in your safe little world of protocol and propriety."

Surprising her, **his** strong, white teeth glistened

amidst the darkness in the semblance of a smile. "You won't last the year, Abbie Dennis."

She answered his smile. "I'll prove your prophecy wrong, Cody Strawhand."

He laughed, his gaze suddenly tender. "I think I'd better get you home before I decide to forget that you're a married woman."

Chapter 5

IT WAS THE MIDDLE OF NOVEMBER AND THE LAST OF
Indian summer, just before the perfect fall days
gave way to the harsh winter. Indian summer.
The words conjured up beauty and mystery and
romance. And Cody Strawhand. She couldn't
stop thinking about him.

He wasn't the average man next door. There
was a charisma about him—the way children
clung to him, adults deferred to him, women
watched him. She sensed that he must have
overcome tremendous obstacles to rise to his
position of importance in the art world, social
prejudice being the least of them.

She folded the last of the Idaho Pink Beans
burlap sacks that Orville had donated for the
day's outing and placed it on her desk with the

rest. She couldn't have chosen a better day to pick juniper seeds. The curio stands along the highways had given her the idea. Why couldn't the children make necklaces out of dried seeds and glass beads and sell the finished product themselves? Dalah had already agreed to take the finished necklaces along with her hand-woven blankets into Tuba City for consignment there.

Persuading Miss Halliburton had presented more of a problem. "You can't possibly watch thirty-four children, Mrs. Dennis. They'll run wild. They could get hurt or lost."

"Give me a chance."

The woman relented, but Abbie suspected that the principal was almost waiting with baited breath for her predictions to come to pass. Transportation had presented another problem. Getting thirty-four children back into the canyons where the junipers grew thickest could never be accomplished in the government Jeep. But then Abbie had what she thought of as a brilliant solution: They could take the old springboard wagon.

True, driving a team of obstinate burros was beyond her capability. But Robert . . . More than once at recess, when she had panicked and thought that he had run away again, she had discovered that the child had wandered off to the corral by the shed to watch the malodorous burros. The indifferent creatures even suffered his caressing strokes. Surely Robert could hitch the burros to the wagon, and probably drive them, as well.

He indicated as much when she asked him, using charades as a last resort in the face of his blank look. The brief crimping of his lips told her that he had understood. She felt a tremendous sense of achievement in having solved two problems at once—transportation and Robert's refusal to get involved.

Miss Halliburton sailed majestically into the room, and the children sprang to their feet, eager to be off. "I hope you know what you're doing, Mrs. Dennis. The responsibility you are assuming?"

"Yes. I've even placed an order for boxes of coral beads from an outlet in Taiwan."

Miss Halliburton's narrow lips, bereft of lipstick, twitched in exasperation. She fixed gray brown eyes that resembled ball bearings on Abbie. "You mean Kaibeto will be palming these necklaces off as genuine handmade Indian articles?"

Abbie tried to smile. "Well, they will be handmade by the Indians."

Miss Halliburton's choleric expression indicated that she saw no humor in the remark, but before she could put forth another argument to block the field trip altogether, Abbie pointed to the tall boy in the back of the room and said, "Wagon, please, Robert."

The boy bolted from his desk and sprang past Miss Halliburton like a contestant in the fifty-yard dash. The old woman grabbed at her wig as if she expected a backwash of wind to blow it off.

"Children," Abbie admonished, when all of them began bobbing from their chairs, "form a single line."

"Don't say I didn't warn you, Mrs. Dennis," Miss Halliburton said and stalked from the room.

In the shed Robert deftly harnessed the two scurvy old burros and hitched them to the wagon. The children all scrambled for a place in the wagon bed that was blanketed with musty hay. Abbie climbed up beside Robert. Julie Begay, who had developed a case of adulation ever since Abbie's wild drive into Tuba City, camped on Abbie's other side.

For more than an hour the wagon bumped over a narrow rutted road that wound back through a red-streaked, sheer-cliffed canyon. The children's laughter amplified with each steep dip and perilous curve of the road where the wash dropped away far below, but Abbie found her hand clutching Julie's bony knee.

She exhaled a pent-up breath and managed a weak smile for the children when Robert halted the wagon in a box canyon studded with gray green junipers. With bean sacks in hand, the children spilled out of the wagon and took off for the trees, scrambling under their low branches to collect the seeds.

Their squeals of delight at escaping the stuffy classroom on such a gorgeous afternoon echoed up and down the canyon. The pungent aroma of piñon and juniper scented the air. A light breeze, carrying the promise of winter, rustled through

the needle-leafed trees. Bees droned over a patch
of sunflowers. Nearby the burros cropped con-
tentedly at the clumps of grass that thrust through
the rock's crevices.

A glorious day! Abbie would have liked nothing better than to stretch out on the shale-bedded
slope and watch the meringue kisses of clouds
that floated above. But, alas, only children had
that privilege. She had to be content to sit and
watch the children dart from beneath the trees
like little field mice.

Contrary to Miss Halliburton's dire predictions, the field trip was going without a slip-up.
No casualties. No arguments. Only happy grins
and sacks that were filling rapidly with seeds.
Abbie was so pleased with the successful outing
that she postponed the return trip for a full
half-hour until the sun tiptoed atop a mesa that
resembled an Indian woman's flounced skirt.

Abbie never knew what caused the burros to
take off with the wagon as if the starting bell had
rung at the Kentucky Derby. The children
claimed it was the *tchindee* spirits. Abbie suspected it was the bees she had heard humming earlier.
Whatever, the braying of the burros grew fainter
with each passing moment. Mary, Delbert, Julie,
Joey, Wendy—all the children's eyes turned to her
as they waited for her wise counsel. All but
Robert. He simply set his face toward the east.
Abbie wanted to comfort him, because she knew
he sensed that it was his fault the burros had
bolted, that he should have secured the reins. But

it would never have done for him to admit weakness before the other children.

She sighed. "We had better start walking back, children."

When would she ever learn to wear sensible shoes in this abysmal terrain? She turned her ankle more than once, and only Julie's quick little hands kept her from sprawling like a rug. Off came the high heels.

The canyon's walls cast eerie shadows, but visions of a wrathful Miss Halliburton were even more frightening. Abbie could only hope that the children knew the way back. What if, in the dark, a child stepped off into the void of one of the deep washes? She cringed at the image of a sheer drop-off, a wayward step. Her fear of heights went to work, her stomach churning at each rolling pebble.

Soon a chill settled like a mist over the canyons. The children would get colds. The faint clip-clop of hooves reached her ears. "The burros!" she breathed. Ahead of her Leo Her Many Horses let out a war whoop of joy.

Abbie's own joy was short-lived when the silhouette of a horseman came into view. The beam from his flashlight temporarily blinded her. Sudden exclamations in Navajo erupted from the children, and she recognized Cody's deep voice reassuring them. Damn! One more reason to justify his judgment that she didn't belong at Kaibeto.

He reined in the Appaloosa alongside her. His

flashlight's peripheral glow illuminated his mocking grin. "If it isn't Moses and the lost tribes wandering in the wilderness."

She checked her rush of grateful words. "Your humor is ill-timed. I suppose everyone is out looking for us?"

Beneath the brim of his hat his eyes laughed at her. "No, only Orville in his Packard. He persuaded Miss Halliburton to let the two of us search before she called out the tribal police, the BIA search heliocopters, the Arizona Highway Patrol . . ."

Abbie groaned. "Say no more, please."

He didn't. He leaned over and, before she realized what was happening, caught her by the waist, pulling her up into the saddle to sit sideways in front of him. "Shall we go back and face the music?"

"I don't think music is what I'm going to be hearing," she said, her dejected laughter muffled against his denim jacket. She encircled his waist for support with one arm while her free hand tugged, to no avail, at the skirt that had ridden high up on her thighs.

Like the Pied Piper, Cody, astride the horse with her ensconced in the crook of his arm, led the children down out of the canyons. The children loved the adventurous trek. And Abbie— she tried not to let herself think or feel anything during that odyssey. But it was impossible, with Cody's hand resting tantalizingly just below her breast. Beneath her thigh she could feel the hardness of him. He wanted her . . . but did he even like her? She doubted it. His contempt was too often evident.

In an effort to redeem herself, she tried to explain the circumstances that had caused the predicament into which she had gotten herself and the children. "With the profits the children make from selling the beads, we can take a field trip into Flagstaff come spring. Just think, these children have never seen a train or a plane or a supermarket. . . . But now I'm afraid that the Dragon Lady will cancel the trip."

Above her head his low chuckle fanned her hair. "I'm sure you'll carry through with aplomb, Abbie Dennis."

He began to talk of other things—to take her mind off the coming confrontation with the principal, she suspected. "Did you know, Abbie, that the juniper berries, because of their pungency, are used to flavor gin?"

She shook her head in a negative gesture. Against her cheek she could feel the strong beat of his heart.

"The name gin," he continued lightly, "comes from the old French word for juniper, *genièvre*—a glass of which you will, no doubt, have need of when we get back."

Foolishly, she wished the ride could continue forever. She told herself that it was only because she wished to postpone the inevitable meeting with Miss Halliburton.

All the lights in the school buildings blazed.

And the Dragon Lady was waiting on the school porch, arms akimbo, when Cody rode into the fenced-in grounds.

With a shudder, Abbie told Marshall about the nightmare of the field trip when he took her up on her invitation for coffee the next day. "The worst," she lamented, "is that Miss Halliburton has written me up for the incident. It won't take many such blots on my record before I'm relieved of my duties."

"As long as she doesn't file the report with the BIA in Gallop, you'll be all right. I might remind you, Abbie, that you still have the rest of your two-year contract to convert her opinion." He stirred cream into his coffee. "Why do you stay, Abbie?"

"I'm not sure," she said with a strained smile. "Maybe because I want to prove that Abbie Dennis can function just as easily as Mrs. Brad Dennis. Maybe just to prove that Abbie Dennis *does* exist. But I won't give up. No matter how badly Miss Halliburton wants me to leave, no matter what kind of incompetent Cody Strawhand thinks I am, no matter how much you yourself try to persuade me of the futility of my efforts."

"I think I'm becoming glad you don't listen to me."

She passed off the indirect compliment. "And you? Why did you come to Kaibeto, Marshall?"

He took another swallow of coffee. His freckles were as pale as the diluted liquid. "My wife took our daughter and left. I was with an international division of a food company. Moving from country to country, living in dirty cities like New Delhi or Teheran. It wasn't the executive wife's life she had in mind when we graduated. And, to do her justice, not many of the marriages in international divisions last. I could have applied for a stateside job—a big desk, long lunch hours, country club membership. But to me the benefits glittered like fool's gold. There had to be more to life."

"And is there?" His answer was important to Abbie.

He shifted and crossed his ankle over one knee. "For me—yes, there is. The beauty and simplicity of this land and its people. Where else do you see such kaleidoscopic sunsets and rainbows that are doubled and tripled?" An embarrassed grin at his impassioned speech spread across his face. "At least here I'm not suffering bleeding ulcers and tension headaches. Two of the side benefits— along with people like you, not to mention your coffee."

Abbie needed more than coffee when she picked up her mail the following week at the trading post, which besides serving as the Kaibeto post office also passed as a bank, though none of the local Indians possessed checking accounts. The envelope was marked with the State of Pennsylvania's return address. Slowly she unfolded the legal-size sheets. For long moments she stood at the counter, staring at the blurred words.

"Bad news?" Orville asked.

She looked up at the kindly old man. His mustache drooped like her spirits. He wore the same baggy, rumpled pants, along with a ragged, faded mulberry red sweater. "I'm a Ms. now." Her trembling hands passed him the sheaf of papers. "My husband—we're divorced."

It was something she had been expecting. But now that it had happened—the finale after twenty years—it was like a blow to her stomach, taking her breath away, hurting.

She could never have filed for divorce herself. Maybe it had something to do with all those Sundays when her parents made her sit quietly on the pew between them. Brad had done the kindest thing, ending the marriage for her. Still, the dissolution of twenty years of joy and tears and anger and laughter . . . she hadn't been prepared for it. She felt as if her lifeline had been cut and she were now adrift in the midst of fifty-foot waves.

Orville passed the papers back with a "hmmmph" that fluttered his mustache. "Looks like you got the short end of the stick, gal."

"I didn't want anything," she whispered. "I'd already had too much of everything."

"But not enough of love, eh?" She looked at him in surprise. "'Pears you're better off. We need to toast your new marital status."

She wanted only to go back to her apartment and crawl into bed for the rest of the day, but it would be too rude of her to turn Orville down.

He bent down behind the counter. "Blast it." His voice was muffled. "That's what I always hated about owning a trading post—can't sell liquor on the reservation. Thought I had some whiskey stuck away. Must have finished off the bottle last year when Cody sold that piece to the Kansas Art Collection."

The old man's head shot up above the counter. Beneath the bushy snow-white brows his blue eyes were bright. "That's it! Cody's got some liquor stashed away. Gin or rum. Maybe both. Doesn't matter. Anything'll do for a divorce celebration. Right?"

She hesitated. She didn't want to hurt his feelings, but the last thing she wanted to do was to celebrate something that had failed. And especially not with Cody Strawhand.

Orville grabbed her hand. "Come on, gal, time's a'wasting." He pulled her along behind him. At the door he grabbed the "Open" sign and flipped it around to "Closed."

"But it's not six o'clock yet," she protested. "You shouldn't be clos——"

"Hell, it don't have to be six o'clock to lift a glass. I oughta know that. Why do you think I'm living in this godforsaken area? Lifted too many glasses." He chuckled as he shut the door behind him and kept walking; she had already learned that no one ever locked a door at Kaibeto. "I banished myself to the least likely place where I would find a drop of liquor. But this, gal, is a special occasion."

He was so excited that she hated to dampen his enthusiasm. Maybe, with any kind of luck, Cody wouldn't be there.

Her luck had apparently run out. Cody met them at the front door. Like the first time she had come to his house, he was bare to the waist. His dusky skin gleamed like polished copper. A towel was thrown over his shoulder, and his hair glistened with water drops.

"If you're going anywhere, Cody, call it off." Orville stalked past him. "Get out the booze. We're having ourselves a party tonight."

Cody cocked a brow at Abbie. Her hands fidgeted in her skirt pockets. She felt compelled to explain. "Orville decided . . . I was . . ."

"She got her divorce papers today," Orville yelled from the kitchen. Doors could be heard banging and pans rattling. "Where on God's green earth do you keep your firewater, Cody?"

"In here," Cody called without taking his eyes from Abbie.

She felt miserable. Miserable about her divorce, miserable about being with other people, miserable about the way Cody was looking at her, as if he could see the hurt that beat a tattoo in her heart. There had to be a way she could back out gracefully from the unpleasant situation. "Really, I'd rather go on back ho——" She had no home now. Wrong, Kaibeto was her home.

She felt the tears that stung her eyes. And felt Cody's hand on her upper arm. He propelled her toward the sofa. "Stay," he said simply. She felt incapable of making any decision at that moment and watched as he crossed to a hutch and took out a bottle of expensive scotch. She liked the way he moved, his grace that could in no way be associated with femininity. He was pure masculinity, raw sexuality.

Orville rambled into the room and headed for one of the deep leather-tufted chairs in the far corner. "Make mine a double, Cody. I never did celebrate my last divorce properlike."

"How many times have you been married?" she asked the old man.

He tugged at his mustache. "Well, let's see. Six, maybe seven. Not rightly sure, gal."

She had to smile. The drink Cody handed her made the smiling easier, though its undiluted strength burned her throat raw. She smothered a choking cough while Orville launched into a humorous accounting of his many marriages and divorces.

"My last wife—she weighed nearly three hundred pounds and could knock the stuffing out of me—ate me out of house and home. That was the last time I took up drinking. When I started drinking more than she could eat, she left me, praise the Lord."

Cody sprawled at the other end of the sofa, listening, saying little as Orville continued to entertain them. Abbie found herself grateful to the old man. He was making the evening easier for her. When Cody handed her another drink, she shook her head. "I really must get back."

"Drink it," Cody said quietly. "The night will be a long, lonely one."

She knew that he was right and also that she

didn't want to be alone with her thoughts, so she sipped the scotch and listened to Orville, who began to nod intermittently between the rambling of his stories. At one point, she decided that she really had to go back to the apartment, that six-thirty would come too early the next morning. But Cody was talking to her, asking her about her marriage.

"I don't know," she found herself saying honestly. "I don't know if I ever really loved Brad, if maybe it wasn't just infatuation, but still . . . the divorce . . ."

"Any divorce forces you to feel a certain amount of self-recrimination, self-blame."

Surprised by the gentleness in his words, she looked up into his face. It was out of focus and nearer her own than it had been a moment ago. "What caused you to leave him, Abbie?"

She looked down into the amber liquor in her glass which had somehow mysteriously refilled itself. "It wasn't anything momentous," she murmured. "I guess it was the high school class reunion that finally triggered everything."

As she had looked around the lavish hotel ballroom at her classmates, she had realized that she represented the epitome of success. Her clothes were the chicest. Her looks—well, if anything, she looked better than the day when she both graduated and married Brad. And her mind hadn't atrophied as some others' had. Having the twins that first year hadn't stopped her from finishing college. Raising Jason and Justin had only postponed her graduation; by the time she received her B.A., Brad had been practicing law for three years.

"I had worked hard to be the perfect mother, the perfect wife," she continued in a voice softened by introspection. "Yet the night of the class reunion I felt no triumph, no satisfaction."

She had felt only an emptiness that had gnawed at her the rest of the night, an emptiness that she had been feeling, but not acknowledging, for years. "The next morning I left with only what I could carry in a suitcase."

Where had their marriage gone wrong? The question lingered on the tips of the tongues of everyone who had known them. They had been the perfect couple. Only Abbie had known that they were far from perfect. They had achieved their goal—Brad's successful career; her place in society; a showplace of a home; two handsome, intelligent sons—but at the expense of their emotional growth.

Oh, Brad had been willing to continue as they were . . . though he had been honest enough not to dissuade her from leaving with words of love. Hadn't they both worked too hard to jeopardize everything by a divorce? he reasoned. What would everyone think? And what about the twins?

But the boys had gone off to college the year before. They were on their own now. And she— was she undergoing the empty-nest syndrome? She doubted it. She was wise enough to recognize that for twenty years of marriage she had been emotionally stymied.

She leaned her head against Cody's shoulder. "Have you ever been married, Cody?"

"No," he said shortly. "My parents were divorced. Their marriage was hell. They came from two different environments."

He knew he was talking too much, but the bitterness wouldn't stop. "Like most Indians, I was torn between bettering myself or being a Navajo . . . torn between two worlds. I never found a woman from either world who . . ." He swallowed the last of the scotch in his glass. His third or fourth drink, he wasn't sure. He was only sure that he had wanted to drown his desire for this woman.

He thought of her too often . . . the way she smelled, fresh and clean, without the cloying sweetness of some women's perfume; the way she looked him in the eyes when she spoke instead of fluttering her lashes and teasing as others did; the innocence in her eyes, as if after all these years she were still a virgin, a novice to the ways of a man and a woman. And yet there was the way she had responded to him the night he brought her home from Dalah's house. It had surprised her, he was sure, as much as it had surprised him. He hadn't expected the heated sensuality that ran beneath the glacial exterior.

And then there was the wariness in her eyes, in her manner, that made him want to protect her, to tell her that everything would be all right.

What a bunch of garbage that was . . . because she wouldn't be all right with him. Another drink and he would take her into his bedroom, and all that innocence in her eyes would be destroyed. He wanted to make love to her. He wanted to keep her there with him, to listen to her soft, melodious voice, to understand the intricacy of her mind . . . and to intimately explore the beauty of her body.

Holy Mother, but he was drunk. Across from him Orville was snoring like an asthmatic walrus. Next to him, half-reclining against him, Abbie stirred, her hand falling lightly on his thigh. He smothered a groan. She didn't know what she was doing to him—or the dangerously thin wire she was walking.

Laughter bubbled low in her throat. "I thought Indians got drunk easily."

"They do." *I am.*

"Strawhand. That's a funny name."

He grinned. "No funnier than Jones or Smith if you say them a couple of times over."

She tilted her head, as if considering the validity of his statement. Her eyes closed. "Jones, Jones, Jo . . ."

His mouth brushed hers, and her eyes flew open. "No," she whispered.

"Yes." He kissed one lid closed, then the other. "You need to be loved."

He showered kisses over the face she turned up to him. But it was her lips, sweet and soft and tremulous, that his mouth kept returning to. The last time he had kissed her—he knew it had been a long time since she had been kissed like the sensuous woman she was. A long time since she had been held as a woman should be held. When his hand slipped down from her shoulder and encircled her waist to pull her over atop him, the slight way she trembled—her almost inaudible moan—told him that it had been a long time since she had found fulfillment. Her husband was a fool. Her ex-husband.

One part of him delighted in the knowledge that she was no longer married but free. Another part whispered that he was a fool to be thinking the way he was, to want her the way he did. She had her world which she would go back to, a world he had lived in and ultimately rejected.

Yet all the rationalization didn't help. Not with her breasts pressing into his chest and her hips shifting against his. He groaned. The hard core of his want for her filled his jeans and throbbed against her soft stomach. He scooped her into his arms and staggered upright. "You're heavy, Abbie."

Her sleepy laughter tickled his neck. Somehow he found the bedroom and the bed. He rolled over atop her, marveling in the wonder of her slender body beneath his own much larger one. He could crush her. But he wanted only to love her. And not for just that night only. "Abbie," he whispered, wanting to hear her marvelous voice, to hear her say she wanted him.

"Ummmm?"

He raised himself up on one elbow to look at her. Her champagne hair was spilled out on the bed about her head. Her eyes were closed. A dreamy half-smile curved her lips.

"Hell," he muttered, "I think I'm too drunk, anyway. Walk in beauty, Abbie Dennis."

Cody sat at the edge of the bed, his head in his hands. His groan awoke Abbie. Her eyes opened, then snapped shut against the blast of sunlight from the arched window opposite the king-size bed. Her head fell back onto the pillow. Oh, no! School was in progress!

Cody rose from the bed in one motion. "I think I may live!"

Once more her eyes opened, this time to mere slits as she eyed the tall, lean man silhouetted against the sunlight. He stretched, his body moving in the marvelously coordinated rhythm of a man in excellent physical condition. His skin was all one shade, a warm toast brown unmarked by a swim suit's white line of demarcation. He turned toward her, uninhibited by the obvious proof of his desire.

Quickly she looked away. "How did I . . . er . . . get undressed?"

"I undressed you."

"What . . . did . . . did anything . . . happen last night?"

His eyes narrowed as he surveyed her. The sheet did nothing to hide the curves of her body, only accentuated them. Her chin was tilted imperiously, her lashes shielding her eyes. Was she returning once more to the grand lady? He leaned across the bed and grasped her chin, turning her face toward him. "If anything had," he said with barely controlled politeness, "you can bet you'd remember."

Which was not entirely true. After he had removed the dove gray skirt and blouse, her slip and bra, his passion had gotten the best of him. A rakish smile lifted the corners of his lips as he vaguely recalled tracing a stretch mark with his fingertip, tracing it all the way to the downy nest . . . and the delicate folds his finger found there. Fortunately for her royal highness, the scotch had gotten the best of him shortly thereafter.

"Get your clothes on. I'll run you back to your apartment."

Orville was still snoring when Abbie and Cody left. On the ride back to the boarding school she kept to the far side of the pickup. A slow heat stole over her as she recalled the way she had wantonly pressed herself against him. That much she too vividly remembered. What else had happened? And what must he think? That because she was divorced she was up for grabs?

Why would he think any differently? Every time she was alone with him, it seemed, she all but threw herself at him. It was quite clear that she wasn't ready for the fast-paced single life.

The pickup slid to a halt in front of her apartment. She turned to him. "About last night . . . it was a mistake—"

"Your coming to Kaibeto was a mistake." *My wanting you is a mistake. Oil and water can't mix.* "You're out of your environment, lady."

She slammed the pickup door. "Not if I have anything to say about it!"

Chapter 6

A DISMAL DRIZZLE SLID DOWN THE WINDOWPANES. The indoor recess would be as good a time as any to start the children working on the necklaces. She pulled out the boxes of coral beads that she had ordered and began passing them out among the restless students.

With a display of aloofness, Robert grudgingly accepted the box she placed before him. When no reprimand for the runaway burros had been forthcoming from her, he had gradually fallen into the school routine, but always with a show of reluctance, as if he were afraid of fully trusting her.

She herself had received a reprimand, the latest in a series. This one had been for being late to report to class duty. How could she adequately

explain to the spinster, Miss Halliburton, that she
had been celebrating a divorce? Or that she had
slept in another man's bed? And, oh, that hang-
over! She remembered the bag of cement that had
dropped inside her head when she had bent over
to slip on her pantyhose.

It seemed that she wasn't really doing too well
as Abbie Dennis, the woman.

Her role as wife was officially terminated, but
the role of mother . . . She picked up the letter
from Justin that lay on her desk. With the enthusiasm that marked everything he did, he had written of his latest girl friend. He would be spending
Thanksgiving with her parents, and Jason was
planning on visiting the home of a football buddy
for the holiday weekend.

She stifled a sigh. It was the weather that made
the day so depressing. And the knowledge that
everyone else was going away for the holidays:
Becky to stay with her boyfriend; Linda and her
baby to visit her parents; Marshall to see his
daughter.

Abbie decided that she would simply accept
Dorothy Goldman's invitation to have turkey
dinner with her the next afternoon and make
every attempt to enjoy herself. But the four-day
weekend stretched out interminably.

Thanksgiving dinner the next day seemed just
as interminable. Abbie sat in Dorothy's cramped
apartment, a showplace for all the salt shakers
and cellars the old woman had collected, and
listened to her talk about the past. "Oh, my, yes,
indeed. I've been a widow for thirty-five years

now. After Tom died"—her plump little fingers fidgeted absently with a salt shaker shaped like a lamp—"well . . . teaching was all that was left for me—and this collection that Tom and I started. Now just look at this one, Abbie, dear. Notice the initials engraved on the shaker's bottom. Some experts claim that . . ."

Nothing to look forward to but retirement—and collecting salt cellars. The prospect of such a bleak future appalled Abbie. After dinner she walked back to her apartment feeling terribly lonely as cottonwood leaves swirled about her. Dejectedly she jammed her hands into the pockets of her alpaca sweater. The sight of Joey Kills the Soldier sitting on her porch with his chin propped on one fist cheered her considerably—and concerned her, too.

"Joey, what is it?" She knelt beside him. "Why haven't you gone off with your family for the holidays?" Most of the children had left the dormitory—except for the usual few, Robert Tsinnijinnie among them. She could count on him to be more recalcitrant than normal come Monday morning and the return of classes.

Joey Kills the Soldier's raisin black eyes crinkled in a smile. "I wait for you." His stubby finger pointed toward a flatbed wagon outside the perimeter of the school fence. An Indian wearing a tall, sugarloaf black hat sat on the wagon's seat, holding the reins. Next to him, wrapped in a plaid wool blanket, sat a ponderous Indian woman. "You go with us, eh, teacher?"

"Where, Joey?"

His brow knitted as he tried to find the English word he needed. A broad grin spread across his moon-shaped face. "Sing."

"Ahh, you want me to go with you and your parents to a Navajo sing?"

Joey nodded vigorously.

Why not? she thought. Why spend Thanksgiving night sitting home alone? "All right. I would love to." She let him take her hand and pull her along behind him to the waiting wagon.

His parents dipped their heads once in acknowledgment of Abbie. With Joey beside her, she slid onto the back of the wagon, her legs dangling over the side along with his shorter ones. What did it matter if the bed's wooden splinters put runs in her cranberry-colored charmeuse dress? It was worth it just to be going to a sing, just to be enjoying herself for the evening.

The wagon lumbered over a corduroyed road much like the one she and the children had taken the day of the seed-gathering, except that it wound further back and upward so that walls of soaring evergreens canopied the wagon. The black velvet night hid the rocky precipices that bordered the rutted road, which was just fine with her. She was able to relax and laugh with Joey as he swung his legs in tempo with hers.

Soon a different tempo could be heard, that of drums and tortoiseshells combined with a muted chant, eerie and mysterious. She wrapped her arms about herself as protection against the night's seeping chill. The wagon rounded a ragged promontory to roll into a small canyon lit by a blazing fire. Like the bonfires of college, she thought, and looked forward to its welcoming warmth. Its leaping light illuminated the many pickups, wagons and battered automobiles that banked the clearing. Within the clearing shadowy figures bobbed and dipped and swayed to the repetitious beat of the music. Bells tied about the dancers' knees provided a rhythmic counterpoint to the drums' insistent thumping.

By the time Joey's father halted the wagon between a 1937 Ford pickup and a burro, Abbie realized that there had to be at least five hundred people at the sing, standing and sitting and dancing. She and Joey followed his parents across the parking area littered with tin cans and beer bottles and shouldered their way through the spectators in search of a place near the front to sit.

In one area a fire dance was in progress, with the dancers' bodies painted white with clay to ward off the heat as they raced around the blazing bonfire. Here and there an Indian tipped a bottle of beer or the ubiquitous *tiswin,* corn whiskey made in stills hidden in the back canyons. The sight of the families, the close-knit clans, celebrating stabbed Abbie with loneliness.

But would she have been any happier if she were still married? Brad would no doubt have been half-drunk, snoring on the sofa after the large dinner that she usually worked all morning on. The twins, in their earlier teens, would normally have spent the afternoon sledding on fresh-fallen snow. Last year they had gone deer-hunting —and she hadn't relaxed until the two had walked through the door, grinning with triumph at the racks of antlers they produced from behind their backs.

She would just have to realize that every period in one's life required time for adjustment. No, she wouldn't go back, she wouldn't reverse her decision to leave Brad if she had it to do all over again.

She let Joey tug her along to another area where men and women danced together. Joey's parents found a spot where they seated themselves, crossing their legs Indian fashion, to watch the dance. Joey pulled Abbie down on the ground between him and his parents. On the far side of the fire men furnished the music by beating a cottonwood drum and singing. Before her the women, all dressed in skirts of intense colors and wrapped in blankets, held to the rear waistband of their partners' trousers. The men simply stood and pivoted while the women danced backward in a circle around them. Abbie could only dub it a cross between an Irish jig and a double shuffle.

During this time small bowls began to circulate around the group. "*Penole* and *piki*," Joey told her. The words meant nothing to her, but she knew that as a courteous guest she would have to partake of the bowl when it reached her. With the greatest reluctance she followed the actions of Joey's parents and dipped her fingers into the bowl, coming up with a glob of some pastelike mixture. It left a cornmeal taste on her tongue.

"Good!" Joey said.

"Good!" she laughed.

The music altered subtly. The rattle of the tortoiseshell and the beat of the drum took on a more primitive rhythm. The couples began to move in an arm-in-arm promenade, their steps fitting their own preference. There was a barbaric splendor about the sight . . . the firelight dancing over the participants, the fierce gazes of the men, the shyer ones of the women.

Then, only a few feet away, between the shoulders of two dancing couples, she saw Cody. Looking up at him, smiling, was Dalah. Cody's dark eyes left Dalah's upturned face to meet Abbie's startled gaze. Beneath the flannel headband the mesmeric quality of his eyes riveted her until a man's body moved between them and broke the contact.

She was shaken. That breathtaking intensity washed over her as it had the first time she had met him at the trading post. It was a primeval feeling that left her weak when she was at last released from Cody's extraordinary magnetism. She tried to focus her attention on the dancers before her, but as the couples ebbed and flowed and another dance began she became aware only of the man who loomed over her. Refusing to give in to his compelling gaze, she made herself watch the new dancers who moved into the circle of firelight.

Cody hunkered down in front of her, blocking her view. His hand rumpled Joey's shaggy hair, and he said something to Joey's parents in Navajo. They nodded in unison. Then his eyes slashed to hers. "This is a squaw dance, Abbie. You must ask the man."

Where had her breath gone? "I . . . the dancing . . . I don't know how—"

Before she could protest, his hands slipped her pumps from her feet. He took her hand and pulled her upright. "Hook your fingers inside my belt," he instructed. "You simply circle around me, always moving backward."

He propelled her into the gathering of couples. The music took up its wild beat. For a moment she hesitated; then, beneath his mocking regard that dared her, she followed the actions of the other women, sliding her fingers behind his belt and slowly moving her feet in a slip-slide fashion. At first she felt self-conscious. Her dress and coloring clearly marked her as an outsider. Then she forgot all as she lost herself in the lure of the savage music.

Cody watched her face, his eyes capturing hers. The very air seemed to scintillate with his sensuality. She swayed against him, and his hand came up to catch her arm.

He drew her out of the circle of dancers and led her away from the fire's brilliant light. Pine needles crunched beneath her feet, but she forgot all about her pumps, left with the Kills the Soldier family. The press of people thinned out, with only an occasional couple talking or walking hand-in-hand as they wandered between the randomly parked wagons and automobiles.

Cody's hand released its grasp of her arm, and

he slid his hands into his jeans pockets. She longed for him to put his arm about her, to feel his warmth again. Like an automaton she fell into step with him, not really caring where they were going. Sometimes they had to circumvent a spiraling pine or twisted juniper.

"Was it Joey's idea to bring you?" he asked.

"Yes." She kept her eyes on the worn path before her. "He told me we were going to a sing."

"It's really a mountain chant. Some call it a windsong, in honor of the promise of spring—the renewal—the wind brings. Did he tell you it's a dusk to dawn affair?"

"No." She glanced up at him shyly. "But I wasn't going anywhere, anyway." She rubbed her hands along her arms. She had been so warm dancing with Cody.

"Cold?"

Not when his eyes burned over her like that. She looked away. "A little."

"The pickup isn't too far off—there, just beyond that buckboard."

"I really should go back."

"Joey's parents don't expect you to."

Her head jerked up. "Why not?"

They reached the pickup, and he leaned over the tailgate and brought out a blanket. "Because I told them I was keeping you with me for the night."

Her lips parted in protest, and he laid his forefinger against them. "Not tonight, Abbie," he said quietly. "No arguing between us tonight. Nothing will happen that you don't want."

She said nothing, merely stood mutely as he draped the soft, fleecy blanket about her, shawllike. "I've been to your world," he said, smiling down at her. "Too often, I sometimes think. Welcome to mine." His head lowered over hers and he kissed her lips . . . a soft, searching kiss that demanded nothing. But when he raised his head, she was breathless with its effect.

"I could do that all night long, Abbie Dennis, but there are other things I want to show you first."

She eyed him warily. Then a small smile gradually ripened her mouth. "I would have to say that this is my first date in twenty years . . . and I'm not quite certain after all this time how to act."

"Forget everything but the essential facts that you are a woman and I am a man and we are here tonight to enjoy ourselves."

He took her hand and began walking back toward the throng of merrymakers. He pointed out a blanket-wrapped Indian off to their left, juggling rounded stones. Ahead a clown burlesqued the priests, dancing out of step, and the children giggled at his antics. She and Cody joined in the laughter before moving on.

Within a stand of evergreens Cody chose a spot bedded with incense-cedar boughs that was close enough to allow them to watch the succession of ceremonial dances but far enough from the pandemonium of the music and celebrating people for them to be completely private. Propped against a cedar, he drew her down beside him and, after tucking the blanket about her feet, nestled her shoulders in the crook of his arm.

"Originally the squaw dances, or mountain chants, were war dances celebrating a victory or a call to battle," he explained, his mouth next to her temple. "Now they're part of a get-together, a social event that sometimes lasts for as many as three nights. It's held in a different place each night, usually fifteen or twenty miles apart."

"Dalah!" she said, suddenly remembering the young Indian girl.

"She came with her family. Because of the isolation of the families, these dances are the only opportunity that many young Navajo women have of meeting and getting acquainted with prospective husbands."

Abbie looked up into the bronze face. "And are you some maiden's prospective husband?" she whispered.

His unwavering eyes held hers. "There is not enough room in my thoughts for anyone but you, Abbie."

She pulled her gaze from his, her senses dazed by the intensity of the passion she read in the depths of his dilated pupils.

Before her passed the dances and legerdemain of the Indian ceremonies, eerie shadows that leaped and bowed. But she was scarcely aware of the performances as she sat there—delighting in the feel of Cody's knuckles nuzzling her cheek, the masculine scent of his skin, his deep, rich voice.

"It is the Navajo goddess of Creation, the

Changing Woman, who created the *Dine'e*—the people," he told her. "She molded them from the skin of the undersides of her breasts." His hand, encircling her shoulder, slid down beneath the blanket to cup the underswell of one breast. Her lids closed. Her breathing seemed to stop. "The tenderest and most sensitive part of a woman's skin, Abbie."

Her breath came out in a raspy, whispery sigh.

One dance faded into another, children grew sleepy and crawled into their mothers' arms, the ancient wandered off to exchange a beer and tales of their youth, while the younger took up the passionate beat of the dance. And Abbie sat spellbound as Cody made slow, rapturous love to her beneath the privacy of the blanket.

While his mouth played gently with her lips, her nape, her ear's shell-like rim, her lashes, his hand tunneled through her hair, loosing the clasp. His fingers dropped to her sweater and unfastened its furry buttons to slide inside her blouse. He caressed the rise of her breasts and dipped lower beneath the wispy bra to discover the turgid nipples. Her head lolled back against the tree trunk, her lashes lying like sable half-moons on her cheeks.

Once more she experienced that sweet, fierce tugging within her that Cody was capable of arousing. She had thought that that part of her— that intrinsic, internal part of her that was supposed to come alive with sensual arousal—had atrophied from disuse. Brad had often cursed her inability to respond. Yet now—now she felt the sweet excitement that was every woman's right when she lay with her man.

Had she ever been so thoroughly kissed? Brad would have kissed her hurriedly—as if the act of kissing was a preliminary that had to be gotten out of the way as quickly as possible. Cody was taking his time, all night, as if it was enough for him just to touch her.

"Cody, kiss me . . . there . . . please."

He released the wispy bra's front clasp to let her breasts tumble free. She lifted one breast, and his head dipped to allow his tongue to gently lave the stiffened nipple. She gasped at the pleasant sensation generated by his mouth that flexed in hungry, sucking motions.

"I want to see you," he said in a voice husky with his passion. "I want to see your coloring." His hand pulled the blanket back, and in the shadow of the trees her breasts gleamed pale white, the aureoles a pale brown, darker where the nipples rose taut and aching. The music beat incessantly, in time with the throbbing within her each time his lips claimed her lips, her nipples. The heel of his hand cupped her beneath her bunched skirt, his fingers rubbing that very feminine area protected by her panties, but not invading. She arched her hips with the music, rolling with the movement of his hand as it rhythmically increased in tempo.

"Cody," was all she whispered when it was over. Tears filled her eyes. Never had anything quite like that happened to her. Cody's only purpose had been the pure act of giving her pleasure. The aftermath left her spent and shaken.

His fingers brushed the tears from her cheeks. "It's all right, Abbie." He gathered the blanket around her and drew her against him.

Just above a mesa the Little Dipper's handle swung out to measure the passing of the night. A soft morning mist floated over land as red as Cody's bandana and baptized the fertile earth. Paprika-colored streaks tinged the dawn sky, reflecting off the pickup's window. The sunrise brought the new day, a day cleansed of old impurities.

Next to Cody, Abbie snuggled deeper in the fleecy gray blanket. She too felt renewed, as if her entire past had been cleansed away. Yet she could not bring herself to look fully at Cody just yet. Past inhibitions warred with the delight that she had found at Cody's hand. Why had Brad withheld that pleasure from her? And yet it was a weakening pleasure, for she found herself wanting Cody all the more.

Cody took his eyes off the dirt road and looked down at her with that half smile of his. "You know, Abbie, I get damned tired of taking you back to your apartment."

Shyly she met his teasing gaze. Her lips unconsciously parted in the smile of a woman who has discovered what it is to feel truly sensuous. "Are you suggesting that I get my own transportation from now on? Perhaps a buckboard?"

He wheeled the pickup into her apartment

driveway and turned to her, laying his arm over the back of the seat. "No, I'm suggesting . . ." He looked down into her upturned face with its provocatively parted lips. He put his finger on the indentation in her lower lip. She was not a woman a man would tire of easily. She knew no cultural or social barriers, only the barrier of herself. Could he hurdle it?

"You know, Abbie, that blanket you're wearing . . . to the Navajo, when a woman wraps herself in a man's blanket it represents the commitment she's making to him. The Anglos call it marriage." His fingers traced the bow of her upper lip. "I want that commitment from you."

She searched his countenance, expecting, hoping, to find humor lurking in his brown eyes or at the corners of his long mouth. She found only the implacable set of his square jaw and the uncompromising line of his lips.

Her face grayed. A fear, similar to the fear she had of heights, churned her stomach. She had just been released from a twenty-year commitment. The thought of surrendering the freedom of her soul again . . . it was like a life-long prison sentence.

"Cody . . . I can't. You ask too much of me."

His lids narrowed over eyes as hard as obsidian. "I won't settle for less. I won't be a diversion for you. An outlet for your pent-up sexual frustrations."

All those years of self-discipline, that proud mask of cool control, exploded in the slap she delivered. He didn't move. The imprint of her fingers against the high ridge of his cheek slowly reddened, and her mouth dropped open at what she had done. She expected instantaneous retribution, but he merely said, "I'm giving you one month to make the decision, Abbie."

"Or what?" she demanded icily.

He leaned across her and opened the pickup door. "Or I'll make it for you."

Inside her apartment she hurled the blanket across the bedroom. Cody and his damn ceremonial marriage blanket! Who was he to issue ultimatums? And yet his threat had been very real. She sensed that he meant to have her. And he was the kind of man who would let nothing stand in his way.

One month. She alternately fretted and fumed about the ultimatum over the following weeks. Cody. She couldn't stop thinking about him. She saw his face in every Navajo child, in every leathery old Indian and wrinkled squaw, in every handsome brave and modest maiden. Those deep, dark eyes that concealed the mystery of life. Those generous lips that promised days of laughter and nights of rapture.

About that one rapturous night, the night of the windsong ceremony, she would not let herself think. His cutting words had unerringly found those feelings about which she was most sensitive. She had trustingly opened herself to him, trying to suppress the inhibitions that had frozen her all those years. And he had used them against her.

No, she couldn't allow his overpowering sensuality to weaken her again. She was resolved to stand on her own two feet, to be her own person before it was too late. Commitments were binding. And she had been wound up with so many commitments that she felt like a spool of thread.

She tried to concentrate on the upcoming holidays. She was attempting to teach the children Christmas carols, and often she would end up laughing when they inadvertently combined "Away in a Manger" with one of their own ritual chants. With their angelic dusky faces with the rosy cheeks and great lustrous eyes they were little cherubs who took her mind off the month that was rapidly running out.

The teachers decorated the school building for the holiday festivities with wreaths of cedar and piñon and juniper berries. Abbie hung up the children's drawings of the nativity scene— invariably mangers set in a desert of red sand. It struck her that this land she found so strange and often unappealing greatly resembled the Holy Land, with its shepherds who watched their flocks by night, and her heart warmed once again to the little shepherds in her classroom—warmed to all but one, churlish Robert.

Excitement ran through the air as the last days before the Christmas vacation approached. Marshall stopped by for coffee and mentioned that he would be visiting his daughter in Oklahoma for the holidays. Jason wrote that he and Justin were going skiing in New Hampshire for the Christmas season.

And herself? What was she going to do?

The week before school let out, she spent the

nights hand-sewing miniature Christmas stockings for her students, stuffing each stocking with a candy cane that she had asked Marshall to buy. She faced a countdown of four days. Surely, she told herself as she worked the needle in and out of the red felt, she and Cody could discuss the issue like two civilized adults.

But there was nothing civilized about passion, was there? Passion, she was discovering, was a primeval, irresistible force, a force that she was not yet ready to reckon with, certainly not when dealing with a man of Cody's sensual magnetism.

When the last day of school arrived, the children were unable to keep still in their seats. They were excited—and she was anxious. Her month was up.

She didn't even attempt to teach that afternoon, but played games with the children. Their favorite—cowboys and Indians. Yet each child refused to play the part of the Indian, because they were not Indians. They were *Dine'e*—the people. She ended up hiding behind her desk, drawing her bow against thirty-four cowboys. Even Robert partook of the merriment. She noticed that he wore a beautifully crafted bracelet of silver and turquoise that was much too large for his thin wrist. The gift for his father that he had been making at Cody's shop?

At last the dismissal bell rang. She lined the children up in front of the classroom door and, as they left the room, handed each the stocking she had made. Most of them shyly accepted the gift and exited. Julie Begay pulled at Abbie's dress until Abbie knelt and then threw dimpled arms about Abbie's neck in a tight little hug.

Delbert bestowed a small smile that gave Abbie hope that perhaps she was succeeding at Kaibeto. Robert jammed his stocking in his jean's pocket and stalked past her. Outside the building parents waited eagerly for their children with burros, buckboards and battered pickups. For some parents this would be the first time in four months they would see their children.

Abbie followed the children out to the steps to see them off, waving at one child, blowing a good-bye kiss to another. She bid good-bye to all except Robert. The boy stood on the steps, his eyes slowly sweeping the grounds. One by one the children went off with their parents until only he was left. Abbie stood behind him, uncertain what to say. Would he understand her anyway?

Thirty minutes passed, yet Robert never moved from his position. The sun was setting, the air growing colder. Still he did not move. She hurt for him. His little face was set as hard as those carved at Mt. Rushmore. She knew that all the tears he choked back were being shed inside his heart. Soon darkness would bring its blanket, and he would have to return to the dormitory with the few other children who had no homes to go to.

What a sap you are, Abbie Dennis. She touched his shoulder. "Robert, you're going to spend the Christmas holidays with me."

She wasn't particularly delighted with her idea, but she just couldn't leave him to spend the holidays alone. Besides, he was the solution to her own problem, albeit a temporary one. Cody couldn't very well demand anything from her when Robert was staying with her. Maybe by the time the Christmas holidays were over her longing for Cody would subside; maybe time would dull his want of her.

The boy remained staring off into the distance where Navajo Mountain dominated the horizon. She touched his arm again. "Robert, come with me."

He looked at her then, and all his resentment flared in his eyes before his lids dropped. Maybe she didn't understand his language, but his resentment—that she understood. He had never wanted to come to the boarding school. It was the *bil'langali'*, the Anglos, who had forced him to leave his father.

Gently she took his wrist and tugged him down the steps, but at the bottom he jerked away. "Now listen, Robert Tsinnijinnie, I have—"

He jutted his head forward and spat, this time aiming—quite successfully—for her face.

She gasped. Incredulity followed by rage swept over her. Her hands balled into fists. The boy tensed, preparing for the coming retaliation.

She smiled, a formidable smile that had often made the twins wince. What she did next was an outrageous thing to do, but the situation demanded something outrageous—so she simply picked up Robert's thrown gauntlet . . . and spat back at him. Shock almost toppled the boy. It was wholly unexpected for a woman to do what she had just done.

Before he could gather his wits about him, she grabbed him by his ear—as she had once promised she would do—and pulled him along beside her. They passed two older students, both girls, who giggled behind their hands. A dull rose tinted Robert's cheeks, but she knew he wouldn't fight her. It would be too degrading for a warrior to fight with a woman!

This time he offered no resistance when she led him over to the dormitory. She knew without being told that it was only a matter of time before he would try to run away again, but this time she doubted he would run to Cody. She sighed as she watched Dalah pack his clothes in a paper sack. She would just have to keep a close eye on the boy.

That evening Robert stood at her apartment window, his hands jammed in his pockets while she fried chicken. Some Christmas, she thought. Neither of them could converse with the other. He resented being there, and she—she had to smile wryly at her predicament—she, who wanted no commitments, had saddled herself with this little savage for the duration of the holidays. She shouldn't have been so impulsive. She had already spent a lifetime paying for her impulsive marriage. Would she never learn?

She forked the last piece of chicken from the frying pan, wondering just how she was going to entertain the child. Hiking? One could only hike so much. Camp-outs? Too chilly now. Besides, he would have to build the fire, and she would bet he would be just stubborn enough to sit there until their faces turned blue.

The front door suddenly opened. Robert was hitting the road already! "Damn!" she muttered and dropped the fork, heading for the living room at a run. She came up short to find Cody standing in the doorway, his hand resting on Robert's shoulder.

Slowly, purposefully, Cody shut the door behind him. He saw the fear, the same mistrust that clouded Robert's eyes at times, leap into hers. He had been foolish, thinking he could demand what had to be freely given. He had spent the four weeks worrying that, like Robert, she too would run, that the holidays would draw her back to her family. He had even asked Orville what he knew of her holiday plans, and that had been a stupid thing to do, because beneath that mop of a mustache the old man's mouth had grinned like that of a kid who had just been let in on a secret.

Even when Orville had confirmed that Abbie would be staying at Kaibeto during Christmas, Cody had known no way out of his dilemma. He couldn't just throw her over his shoulder and ride off as his ancestors had done when they had robbed other camps for brides.

But he wasn't about to walk away without Abbie. He glanced at Robert, who had turned indifferently back to the window. "I see that another man has already claimed you."

She wiped her hands nervously on her apron. "It seems that Robert and I are stuck with each other. His father . . . he didn't come, Cody." She spread her hands. "And there didn't seem to be anything else to do but invite Robert home for the holidays."

Home for the holidays! The idea came to him like a bolt of welcome lightning. It would be a surprise for his father and Deborah, but it would resolve the dilemma he faced with Abbie. He crossed the room toward her. Before she could retreat from him, his hands encircled her waist to untie the apron. "Get your things, Abbie. You and Robert are coming with me."

She clutched at the apron and the fear he had hoped to dispel still lurked in her eyes. "Cody . . . I can't. I can't just up and leave and—"

"You assumed responsibility for Robert, and the boy deserves to celebrate Christmas with his kind, with his people. We're going to New Mexico, to spend Christmas with my parents. Their house—Cambria—sits in the midst of a Navajo rancheria."

She looked toward the boy, and Cody could see that she was vacillating. He wouldn't give her a chance to refuse. "Abbie, my father still sits on the Navajo Tribal Council. If you don't come with me, I'll see to it that pressure is brought to bear on the BIA to question your competency as a teacher."

Her eyes flashed. "You never wanted me here to begin with, so why—"

"But I want *you*. Are you coming?"

Chapter 7

AS MUCH AS HE TRIED, ROBERT COULDN'T HIDE HIS excitement behind his usual impassive facade. The boy's inky eyes glowed like rekindled coals as he stared out the window of Cody's private plane, a Cherokee 235. The four-seater airplane winged its way through the night toward the seventy-six thousand acres that were Cambria.

"All of that is owned by one family?" Abbie asked incredulously.

"At one time Cambria, which belonged to my great-grandmother, was the largest land grant in the United States. Over five million acres." Cody kept his eyes on the instrument panel. "Over the generations portions have been sold off because they were too costly tax-wise. It's still too much for my father to oversee at his age."

Far below passed the pinpoints of lights of Gallop, then Albuquerque; off to the left was Santa Fe. At last they reached the flare-lit dirt strip of Cambria's airport. Cody deftly pulled the yoke back until the stall-light flashed, then eased the plane smoothly onto the runway. Abbie exhaled the breath she had held since they took off from Pulliam Airport at Flagstaff. Flying in a commercial aircraft hadn't ever bothered her, but flying in Cody's small plane had.

When he extended his hand to help her step down from the wing, her legs were trembling so much that she thought her knees would buckle. They did. She collapsed within the warmth of his arms as the chilly December wind whirled about them. "I'm taking the bus back," she muttered against his chest.

"Buses aren't any safer and not nearly as fast," he said, taking the opportunity to kiss her temple where wisps of her hair escaped the clasp.

"I feel like going on my knees and kissing the ground."

He tilted her chin up. "How about kissing me instead, Abbie?"

"You promised tonight that—"

"—if you came with me to Cambria, I wouldn't force you to do anything you didn't want to," he finished, his lips tickling the hollow just below her ear. "But that doesn't exclude persuasive tactics, does it?"

She nodded toward Robert, who stood before them, holding his sack of clothes. He seemed to look right through them. Cody sighed. "Your watchdog." He placed his hand on Robert's shoulder. "Listen, son, we Navajo have got to stick together. It's the two of us against all of her."

The blast of a car's horn interrupted Cody's council of war. Taking the two suitcases, he steered Abbie and Robert toward the four-wheel Blazer that had just driven up. A slender woman wrapped in a white wool coat got out and hugged Cody to her. The wind swirled her sophisticated short-styled hair so that the silver strands that intermingled with the brown seemed to have a life of their own. She stepped back from him, and Abbie saw by the car's lights that the attractive woman was much older than Cody, maybe in her sixties. But her high-planed cheekbones stretched her skin firmly. The woman had to be the stepmother he had mentioned during the plane ride. And his mother?

"Cody," Deborah said warmly, "it's been too long." She turned to Abbie. "And you must be the schoolteacher he told me about on the phone tonight." She took Abbie's hand, and her dark, tilted eyes misted. "We're deeply grateful to you."

"But I did nothing," Abbie said, restraining the impulse to add that she hadn't even wanted to come.

"You're the reason our son came home. That's enough."

"Deborah," Cody admonished affectionately, "it's cold. Please get in the car."

Behind the wheel sat a man whose thick hair

was iron gray. The eyes he turned on Abbie were as dark brown as his corduroy hunting jacket—and as warm. "It's a pleasure to have you as our guest, Mrs. Dennis."

His voice held the same deep resonance as Cody's, and his features were stamped with the same virile power, though he must have been at least in his seventies.

Cody and Abbie sat in the back seat, and Deborah wedged Robert between her and her husband. When the older woman wasn't filling Cody in on Cambria's operations or telling Abbie some of Cambria's history, she was talking to Robert with the low intonations of the Navajo language that continued to baffle Abbie. Sometimes the boy would nod in response to Deborah's questions, but he never spoke. Yet, Abbie noticed that the few times Chase Strawhand addressed him, the boy replied—tersely but respectfully.

In the back seat Cody stretched out his long legs diagonally. His fingers absently stroked Abbie's nape where the clasp bound her hair while he chatted with his parents. At his touch a pleasant shiver raced up her spine. She felt like a dormant seed that would sprout to life when the conditions were just right. He had the power to make her completely aware of herself as a woman, and that was the problem. She didn't know which she dreaded more, which would kill her first: her sickness or his cure.

It was much later by the time they crossed the bend in the Pecos and drove up before the main house. "Cambria's castle," Cody said wryly.

All the house lights seemed to blaze against the night and the isolation, illuminating the heavy earthen wall exterior with its spiraling turrets, dormer windows and wide balustraded verandas. Looking out the Blazer's window, Abbie could sense a strength about the house that had nothing to do with its solid structure. Rather, it possessed a strength of character, like Cody and Chase and Deborah.

Abbie followed Deborah up the wide staircase that was banked with polished mahogany railings. Behind her Cody muttered, "Did I ever tell you what a delightful tush you have, Abbie?"

She flashed him a withering look and glanced at Robert, relieved that the boy didn't fully understand English. But how could he miss the lustful gleam in Cody's eyes?

Deborah turned into a wing of the house that was flanked with doorways. "I'm putting Robert in the room connecting with yours, Abbie," she said, with a sly twinkle in her dark eyes for her stepson.

Cody set Abbie's suitcase down next to the rosewood dresser. His gaze actually seemed to caress Abbie as they stood before the others. "I think Abbie knows that a mere bedroom door wouldn't stop me, Deborah."

"Just as persistent as his father," Deborah sighed.

Cody *was* persistent, though he made not the slightest effort even to kiss Abbie. This only disconcerted her more. She was beginning to

realize that his seduction of her would be through
her senses, rather than from an initial outright
taking of her. *That* she could say no to, but how
could she say no to the way the fever-bright
pinpoints of fire in his eyes burned unashamedly
over her face at the breakfast table, or the way his
eyes scorched her breasts when his gaze happened
to linger on her in the midst of a conversation
with Chase?

His legs touching hers under the table, their
thighs brushing when they rode horseback with
Robert over Cambria's purple escarpments and
low, rolling valleys, his fingers rubbing her sensitive palm as he taught her and a taciturn Robert
how to lasso with a rope—these could not be
ignored or wished away.

She found herself watching the carved line of
his lips, found herself wanting to delineate that
line with her index finger, found herself badly
wanting him to kiss her. By the end of that first
day, even the fine hairs on her arms were so
sensitized that they were like tiny antennae, pick-
ing up the erotic signals that Cody was transmit-
ting.

Christmas dinner that evening was an intimate
affair with only two of the servants from Cambria's rancheria to wait on the elegantly set table.
Robert sat sullenly, but Abbie sensed that it was
his ignorance of the myriad dining utensils that
had prompted his moodiness. But Deborah, who
had taken Robert down to the rancheria that day
to meet the children, was ahead of her. She

ordered a Mexican youth dressed in a white cotton *camisa* and *calzones* to remove all the dinnerware but the knife and fork. After that Robert pushed the roasted wild turkey and cornbread and squash dressing around his plate with his knife and surreptitiously ate when he thought the others were busy talking.

"Our young friend here," Cody said to his father, "is an example of a child caught between two worlds. All the education the federal government provides often fails to bridge the gap—because you still have human emotions to deal with, emotions that can't be programmed."

The wine in Abbie's glass sloshed perilously near the crystal rim. She tensed, sensing that Cody's statement was partially directed toward her, also.

Chase, his black eyes set off by his thick iron-gray hair, replied in sparing but intense words. "Our legislation has accomplished a lot, son, but as far as the progress on behalf of the Indian"—his broad shoulders, still unstooped by time, shrugged—"our people's superstitions and determination to hold to their anachronistic way of life have held them back more than any discrimination on the part of the Anglo."

Abbie could understand why Chase Strawhand had made such an excellent politician and governor. He had neatly addressed the stated issue and ignored the controversial unspoken subtext of the remark.

Deborah smoothly broke the tension, saying in

a light voice that subtly chided them, "Enough of politics, Chase and Cody."

She turned to Abbie. "I'm sure Cody didn't tell you that the president gave a box Cody had made—done in silver and inlaid with malachite and lapis lazuli—to the queen of Denmark."

Cody, casually dressed in a bark-colored sweater and chamois jacket, eyed his stepmother with mild reproval. Without the bandana knotted about his forehead he looked to be a product of Anglo civilization, but Abbie knew that he was more. Only a deceptive veneer of Western culture overlay the fierce, primitive passion of his Indian ancestors.

"What my modest stepmother didn't tell you," he said, "is that her paintings have received recognition from the National Indian Arts Exhibition, among others, and that two are currently on exhibition in a prominent Fifth Avenue gallery."

Abbie remembered the paintings in Cody's house—they were his stepmother's. She felt as if she were gradually discovering the pieces to the puzzle of Cody Strawhand. She reflected on the cultures that he had been exposed to. He must have spent some of his time at Cambria. He must have become accustomed to the Sevres porcelain, Remington bronzes, Chippendale antiques—as well as both the stimulation of Santa Fe political life and the austerity of reservation life.

Each piece of the puzzle only increased her desire to know more, yet she doubted the wisdom of fitting the pieces together. The full picture might be too alluring for her to resist. She should never have agreed to come to Cambria.

She told herself that again the next day when Cody took her through the old stone millhouse. It rose dark and mysterious against the blustery December sky. She pulled her rabbit jacket more closely about her. A musty smell of long disuse enveloped her when she followed Cody into the dim but welcoming warmth of the building.

"The story goes that the old place is haunted," he said as he led her past the giant stone roller and the empty cornmeal bins.

She wasn't superstitious, she told herself. Still, she didn't remove her hand when Cody took it and pulled her up the narrow stairwell. His spurs clinked hollowly on the wooden steps. "The story goes that my great-uncle supposedly hung himself from the mill's rafters when his father prevented him from marrying the woman he loved."

"A charming story," she said dryly. She looked uneasily around her at the paraphernalia of rotten saddles, greasy blankets and worn hides and sheepskins.

Cody loomed before her. Beneath his Stetson's brim his eyes held hers. "But quite true. There are men who will go to any extremes for the women they want."

Insouciantly she brushed the dust off her hands on the back of her denim jeans, but her pulse was beating like a jackhammer at his nearness. "What's on the third floor?"

He grasped her wrists and pulled her hands

against his sheepskin coat. "Abbie . . . you're
shilly-shallying like a nervous filly. There's nothing to be frightened of. Not ghosts . . . not me."

"I'm . . ." Her eyes moved about the room's
dark corners, looking anywhere but at Cody's
face until his hands anchored themselves at either
side of her head and drew her mouth up to his.
His lips played lightly over hers.

"Abbie, I want to love you. Don't shake your
head. Love is something that can be good and
beautiful, if you let it."

"It's just that . . ."

His lips stilled hers. The gentle kiss explained
what he felt his words would not. He pulled away,
his eyes searching deep into hers for any glimmer
of resistance. He found none, but neither did he
find that answering need he wanted of her. There
was simply no flicker of response. He was a man
trained to infinite patience; living close to nature
as a child had taught him that much. He was
accustomed to waiting for the wary approach of
the rainbow trout, the sight of the stag before his
rifle, and he would wait for her.

His fingers found her hair clasp and loosened it
to fan her hair in a mantle of royal gold about her
shoulders. Under his intent regard her lids
dropped. "Abbie," he whispered, his arms easing
her down onto the mound of furry sheepskins,
"forget all your past worries and fears. Today is
different; you are different; I am different."

His lips sought the hollow below her ear. Her
pulse beat furiously there. When his fingers
slipped beneath her coat to undo her western

shirt's tiny pearl snaps, she caught them. "Cody
. . . it's been so long. I . . . with Brad . . . I . . .
I'm afraid."

He kissed away the ridiculous tears that over-
flowed her tightly squeezed lids. His fingers released her bra's clasp and freed her breasts. His
lips slipped down to enclose the soft nipples.
Abbie's gaze was lost in the dark rafters far
above. Her head moved from one side to the
other in a negative gesture of her hopelessness.
What Cody had done before—that one miracu-
lous moment—that was entirely different from
what he wanted now. The joining of the two of
them . . . it could only bring keen disappoint-
ment to them both.

Somehow, even as his hands found delight in
cupping the weight of her breasts, he unzipped
her jeans, though she was not quite certain at
what point he pulled them down over her ankles.
She only knew that some time later her bra, her
panties, her boots—his Stetson, spurs, sheepskin
jacket—were strewn about the two of them like a
fortress . . . and Cody was giving her a tongue
bath that was making her forget all the inhibitions
wrought by the last twenty years.

Her mouth, shoulders, navel, palms, fingers—
even the soles of her feet. He was carpeting her
body with flowers of kisses. Her nipples peaked in
expectant rapture.

"Abbie, you have a beautiful body." His
tongue traced the path of one stretch mark.

"I carried twins," she whispered, her breathing
regulated by her gradually building excitement.

"I tried all the creams to make the marks disappear . . . After a while I gave up . . . I just didn't care anymore."

His tongue flicked a line of disturbing kisses down the bow of her ribs, and she quivered uncontrollably. "It would have been a shame had you succeeded, Abbie." His body half-covered hers; his forefinger stroked the indentation in her lower lip while he talked in a low, quiet voice.

"The Navajo make a *kachina* doll out of a cottonwood tree with a knife and a rasp. These *kachinas* represent supernatural powers. The doll is covered with a light coating of kaolin, a white clay, and left that way for some time. A young girl is like that doll. It is only when the face's characteristics are painted that the doll assumes mystical powers. The same with a woman; only when life has painted her character does the woman achieve the full powers of her femininity."

His words touched her in a way that his kisses and hands had not, deep within. The tension which seemed to have bound her for so long ebbed with the renewal of his kisses. Her legs slackened in languorous abandon as his mouth resumed its tender kissing. His lips softly penned a line of love up the inside of her thigh, ending with the barest brush across the mound of crisp hair that curled against his lips. Her fingers entwined themselves in his thick hair.

"I would mark you as mine, if I could," he said in a husky voice before his mouth reclaimed the soft area of her inner thigh in a kiss *au cannibale*, which he knew would leave a bruise. She gasped and buckled, but rewarded him by clasping his head between her hands and drawing him to her. He kissed gently until he sensed she was ready and then parted her for deeper tongue strokes.

"Cody . . . hurry, please . . . I want you."

He moved up over her, sliding into her with an ease that surprised her. His long hair tickled her eyelids, and she opened her eyes to find him watching her while his body—harder, heavier, hairier than hers—moved in slow, rhythmic strokes. He began to talk to her, something Brad had never bothered to do during his silent and furiously fast lovemaking.

"This month of waiting for you, Abbie . . . I vacillated back and forth. Sometimes I was so angry at your Anglo's cool aloofness that I wildly contemplated coming to your apartment and raping you . . . shocking you into some feeling. And at other times . . . remembering the wariness in your eyes . . . I thought only of holding you through the night . . . of comforting you . . . telling you everything would be all right."

His strokes of love gradually accelerated and still he talked, whispering fantasies of what he would do to her the next time, of all the magical, mystical and marvelous delights of lovemaking. All at once she was gripping his forearms, her fingernails digging into his flesh. Like that night of the windsong, she could sense that laser beam of intense pleasure focusing its powerful thrust at her core.

Cody held her against him, barely moving as he

coaxed the full measure of the moment from her
suddenly rigid body. It happened. Several violent
spasms convulsed her; then her body collapsed
like a rag doll. He gathered her to him and rocked
her. His low voice crooned gentle words in a crazy
mixture of Navajo, English and Spanish.

Soft tears gathered in her eyes. What had
happened the night of the windsong—Cody's gift
of bringing her to that peak of release—carried in
comparison only a modicum of the intense ecstasy
she had just experienced as he had moved inexorably within her.

"I'm so sorry," she wept, too ashamed to look
up into Cody's discerning eyes. "Nothing . . .
nothing like this has ever . . . I didn't think it was
possible for me. . . ."

"Shhh, it's all right, Abbie."

He knew that too often the Anglo male in his
race against time for achievement, for progress,
for recognition, grew accustomed to haste and
sacrificed those precious moments of anticipation
for that fleeting second of finality. He was careful
not to move within her. He didn't want to spoil
her lassitude as he stroked her hair, pulling waves
of it over her shoulder to tickle her highly sensitized nipples.

Through the thicket of her lashes she shyly
glanced up at him. "Cody . . . you—you haven't
. . . ohh." Her lips issued a frustrated sigh. "I've
never felt so inept at words."

He chuckled. "It's our turn together now, my
love."

*   *   *

To discover the stranger in her body was as shocking to Abbie as finding a stranger in her bed. Cody had unmasked the stranger—and the stranger was she. He had liberated her from all her past inadequacies, from all the failures that Brad had subtly attributed to her. Suddenly she was a glutton for sensual experience. The mere way Cody's eyes made unabashed love to her across the dinner table that night set her off all over again.

If Chase or Deborah noticed the sensual communication that flowed between their son and Abbie at dinner, they said nothing. Robert, she was certain, did notice. With a child's fine sense of perception, he felt the tenuous change, the new shading, in her relationship with Cody. His eyes flickered from Cody to her several times before he shuttered his expression.

She puzzled over the boy's continued hostility later that night as she bathed, and she puzzled over her new self. Her whole body was now full of mysteriously secret places . . . the tip of her tongue, the cushion of her fingertip, the hollows behind her knees. In the warm, scented bathwater she considered those places, finding an infinite pleasure in her body. Why had she always feared it?

Yet she was almost afraid to face Cody the next day, afraid to see the condemnation that she would have received from Brad had she demonstrated such a liberated response to his lovemaking. At breakfast she found no condemnation in Cody's dark, enigmatic eyes, but she did detect a reservation within those depths, as if he were awaiting something further.

After breakfast his father asked him to deliver a bale of barbed wire to Wild Cat Camp, one of the three ranch houses on Cambria. Cody took her and Robert with him in the ranch's pickup. The pickup bounced and jolted over unmarked land carpeted with winter grass toward a destination known only to Cody. No trees indicated boundaries, no hillocks or draws hinted at direction. Yet the emptiness of the land offered a freedom that appealed to Abbie. The men and women who had conquered this rough, unyielding land had to have been strong.

Occasionally she slid covert glances at the man who handled the vehicle with such assured control. She knew so little about him. She would have liked to ask him a hundred questions about himself. She wanted to know all the things that had happened to make him the man he was, but she sensed that in many ways he was as closed as Robert was.

Cody pointed out Wild Cat Camp, which consisted of a line cabin that was little more than a shack, a shed and two staked corrals. A mile or so further on he began to parallel a stretch of fence and followed the line for several more miles before a lone horse came into view. Near the roan gelding a young man, his shoulders hunched against the cold, waited. Cody got out and greeted the cowpoke with a tip of his hat and said something Abbie didn't catch; then the two men hefted the bale of barbed wire out of the pickup bed.

She and Robert slid out of the pickup into the arctic cold. Their breath crystalized in the air. The pickup's cab shielded them from the frigid wind while they stood and watched Cody help the rail-thin ranch hand repair a section of fence. After a while Cody came over to them. Hunkering down next to Robert, he slid his big leather gloves onto the boy's smaller hands and explained in Navajo how to tack the wire tautly to the fence post.

Robert hunched down next to the young hand and began tacking. The boy's hair had begun to grow and no longer looked so much like peach fuzz. Watching with Cody, Abbie could see that the boy's face lost some of its sullenness. "You're good with Robert," she told Cody.

The cold wind whipped her hair across her face, and his hand caught the wayward strands to push them back. "He's learning to give of himself, Abbie. Will you?"

Beneath the Stetson's brim Cody's eyes were inscrutable. She looked away, turning her gaze back to Robert. "That depends on what you're asking."

Cody made no reply; instead he moved away to help Robert and the ranch hand finish up the section of fence.

That night, lying on the old-fashioned mattress stuffed with fluffy wool, she reflected on Cody's question. What exactly was he asking of her? More than she was prepared to give?

Her thoughts returned to the previous afternoon when he had made love to her. How strange it was that her union with Brad, legalized by a marriage license, should have seemed so often like debasement. But with Cody . . . he was right, it had been beautiful.

Just as she reached out to flick the bed lamp off, the door opened. He stood there. He wore only his jeans and boots—and the bandana that made him look so untamed. He seemed to be beyond the dictates of civilization that decreed a man's dress, a man's code.

Slowly he shut the door behind him. She didn't try to shield her scanty satin and lace nightgown with the sheet as she would have done at one time, but neither could she meet the directness of his gaze. Her eyes lowered to the expanse of broad, coppery chest and followed the shift and play of his flesh and muscle as he crossed the room to her with that graceful stride.

He leaned over her, one fist planted on the mattress at either side of her hips. "Abbie? Look at me."

She dragged her gaze up to meet his.

"Do you still have"—he paused, as if searching for the right word—"an *isnati?*" He hesitated again, then found the word. "Your monthly flow?"

Crimson flooded her face. "Yes," she breathed.

His eyes had that disconcerting habit of watching her lips. "And are you protected?"

Her breath caught in her throat. "I—after the twins—we wanted more children. But I never became pregnant. It seems that I must not be . . . fertile."

"And if you are?"

"Why are you asking all this?"

"I'm telling you, Abbie, that I want to see your toothbrush next to mine, to find you at my side when I awake in the morning, to argue with you over the brand of coffee you bought . . . silly, mundane things that make up a relationship."

Automatically her hand reached for a packet of cigarettes on the nightstand. Of course, there were none. Whatever had possessed her to give up smoking? "The marriage blanket again," she said dully.

"Yes." It was a flat, harsh sound. "I'm asking for a commitment, not necessarily one made legal by paper, but certainly one of the soul."

She looked off into the room's shadowy corners, where the lamp's light did not reach. "Cody . . . you don't know how much you ask. For twenty years I struggled to be what Brad wanted me to be, and I couldn't do it. I can't make that kind of suffocating commitment to a man again, not for a long time, not until I know me again, maybe not forever."

His hand jerked her chin back toward him, forcing her to meet the ferocity in his gaze. "And in the meantime? What about what happened yesterday?"

"I don't know what you're implying."

"I'm implying that what happened yesterday between us—without a commitment—makes you little better than a whore, my love."

Without thinking, she slapped him. At once she regretted the action. She was appalled at what she had done. Violence had never been part of her nature, but this made the second time she had resorted to violence with Cody. Her eyes widened at the reddened imprint on Cody's jaw—and the fury that burned in his eyes that were now smoke black. His grip tightened brutally on her chin; then abruptly he dropped his hand.

"I think the holidays are over. I'll fly you home tomorrow."

"It was nice of you to run Robert and me into Albuquerque."

Deborah took her eyes off the busy interstate highway long enough to cast Abbie a sympathetic glance. "You're probably right about catching a commercial flight. It will give Cody a chance to cool off."

She returned her attention to maneuvering the car around the curves of the Sangria Mountains. "You know, Abbie, I've found that Cody's passions, like my husband's, run deeper than those of ordinary men."

Abbie stared below them to the undulating foothills that embraced Albuquerque. "I know," she replied in a small, miserable voice. He hadn't even bothered to see her and Robert off that morning. Chase had diplomatically explained that his son had instead ridden out to one of the camps to deliver salt licks and bales of hay for the winter feeding.

"You see," Deborah was saying, "Cody didn't

have a normal child's life." She flicked a glance at
Robert, who sat taciturnly in the back seat.
"Perhaps I shouldn't be telling you this, but I
think it's important that you understand."

Abbie didn't bother to temper her sarcasm. "I
must say, Cody Strawhand is certainly an enig-
ma."

"As the son of New Mexico's governor, Cody
had unique opportunities," Deborah explained.
"He attended the very best schools; he often sat
at dinner tables where there were as many nation-
alities represented as there were guests; he spoke
three languages fluently; he played with the children of diplomats and celebrities and entrepre-
neurs. All this when he was still just a child.

"Unfortunately, the demands on a governor's
social life kept Chase and Christina, my husband's
first wife, from establishing a normal home routine. Rather than run again for office, my husband chose to serve on the Navajo Tribal Council
at Window Rock. That's the Navajo Nation's
capital—like Washington, D.C. I think that by
returning to reservation life, my husband hoped
to give Cody the kind of close family relationship
every child needs. In that way, the decision was a
good one. Cody learned to exist with the necessi-
ties of life alone. You might say my husband was
trying to strengthen his son, to teach him survival
on the most basic level."

"But? . . ." Abbie asked, hearing the reservation in Deborah's voice.

"But the deprivations that Christina faced . . .
well, you can imagine the culture shock she

underwent, leaving the governor's mansion to live in a hogan. Dirt floors, no electricity, no running water. Within the year she left Chase and Cody, who was ten or so, for another politician, a man of her own race that time."

"I see," Abbie said slowly, hurting for the child Cody had been. That explained why Cody demanded all—or nothing.

"Now you can understand why Cody harbors such a deep resentment for the pretentiousness of social roles, why he harkens to the call of the wild places and avoids the upper echelons of society like the plague. He wouldn't even accept his inheritance of Cambria, so his father and I must return periodically to oversee its operation."

Deborah bit her lip to still its trembling, and Abbie said, "You love Cody very much, don't you?"

"Like my own son. He's so very much like his father." She ran slender fingers through her sophisticated short-cut hair. "I wish I had a cigarette."

For the first time Abbie laughed. "You gave up smoking too?"

Deborah grimaced. "Chase never let me get started. I remember the first time I pulled out a package of cigarettes I had found. . . ." She gave a small laugh. "I think I've been rattling on, Abbie. But I like you very much—and I wanted you to understand Cody, if that's possible for anyone."

"Tell me about you and Chase. Please."

"There's not that much to tell. I met him at the

Santa Fe Indian Boarding School . . . and fell wildly in love with him, although I was just six or seven at the time and he was already a senior. Years later, when he was going to the university, he met Christina, and after the war—World War II—he went on to become governor. . . ."

"And?" Abbie prompted. "When did Chase finally come back into your life?"

Deborah hesitated. Those passionate months during the war when she and Chase had been marooned on a Philippine island, that special time, would always be her secret. She said instead, "Following the war we were engaged briefly, but after Chase was elected governor Christina decided she wanted him back. When I learned later that they had divorced, I knew I might never have another chance." She shrugged and smiled self-deprecatingly. "So I stalked him like a female panther."

She glanced in the rearview mirror at Robert, who sat as dispassionately as her stepson had at breakfast. It would be difficult to reach below the child's self-imposed barrier—and Cody's—but love could do it. The beautiful woman beside her was, she felt, capable of giving great love. But would she want to give it to outcasts such as those two?

Deborah risked one last word on the subject. "The way Chase loves me now—the force of his passion and the strength of his love—it was worth those first few years of self-doubt, Abbie. Of wondering if he would take Christina back if she came to him again."

Abbie looked out the window, but she didn't
see the outskirts of Albuquerque slip by, the
modern malls and stuccoed condominiums. Passion. The force of Cody's passion threatened to
overpower her, like a tidal wave. Had she met
Cody when she was younger, perhaps she would
have been equal to it. But now . . . now she had
been conditioned by too many years of repres-
sion, had acquired the debilitating quality of
self-containment. She could no longer give so
easily of herself. She didn't even know if there
was any of her left to give. And that was what was
of supreme importance to her now—to find herself.

She couldn't handle both—the passion she har-
bored for Cody . . . and the passion, the desperate need, to prove that Abbie Dennis still existed.

Yet she could not so easily put Cody from her.
His image was engraved on her mind . . . his
touch and voice on her soul.

Chapter 8

"Swinging by the airport was no problem, Abbie. I had to come down Flagstaff way anyhow. Where did you and Robert go?"

"New Mexico," she answered noncommittally.

Marshall flashed her a glance. As if sensing her unspoken wish, he respectfully refrained from questioning her further.

Politeness compelled her to say something. "I was surprised when the agency told me that you had cancelled your holiday vacation leave."

"An emergency at the Leupp Boarding School came up. That's where I just came from."

Only then did Abbie notice that Marshall's healthy tanned face had a gray cast. "What happened?"

He swung the Interagency Motor Pool's Jeep off Highway 89 onto 160. "Suicide. A ten-year-old hanged herself from a bath stall showerhead."

"Oh, God, no." She thought of Robert sitting stonily in the back seat and was for once glad he didn't understand English very well.

"I don't think the BIA will ever learn that taking an Indian kid to a white boarding school comes as a terrific shock. Like being pushed out of a cozy kitchen into a howling blizzard. Oh, our schools are modern and expensive. And our teachers, the ones like you, really try. But the kids are lonely. They enter confused and bewildered, and they leave the same way. When they enter at least they know that they're Indians. They come out half-red and half-white, not knowing what they are."

She closed her eyes and leaned her head back against the seat. Chase and Cody had fenced on the very issue that Marshall was discussing. The horror of the suicide—it made her feel so helpless, the situation seem so hopeless.

"Is there anything that can be done?" she asked without opening her eyes. She didn't want to see the desolation of the country that was inexorably swallowing up the car. In Albuquerque it would have been so easy to catch a plane to anywhere. Houston, Kansas City, San Francisco. But she wasn't going to run.

"Something *has* to be done," he said hollowly.

"Where would you start, Marshall?"

He was quiet for a moment. "You know, Abbie, we talk about the Indians being culturally deprived." He laughed angrily. "They aren't. You might say that they're the only people in this melting pot who have kept their culture. What have we, the urban white Americans, got? A culture of the mass media that's fed to us."

He shook his head. "I'm going off on a tangent. I'd start, Abbie, by doing away with the restriction that forbids them to talk their language or sing their songs in the boarding schools. Hey, Abbie?"

She opened her eyes. "I wasn't sleeping. Just thinking, Marshall."

"How about thinking about going skiing with me before the holidays are over. The Snow Bowl reported more than seven inches of snow last week."

"Marshall, to be honest, I tried seeing another man this week. And it was no good. I don't think I'm up to mixing with the opposite sex yet." She smiled wryly and added, "To quote Garbo, 'I vant to be alone.'"

"It was that bad, eh?"

She was relieved when he didn't ask her the name of the man she had seen. "That bad."

"When you decide to make the circuit again, Abbie, I hope you'll give me first chance at bat."

Abbie and Dalah tacked the last deerhide Yei mask to the wall above the blackboard. They would have been more appropriate for Halloween, she thought.

Dalah had obtained the masks and the *kachina* dolls from the Navajo Indian Culture Center in

Tuba City the week before. Orville contributed the large, and costly, squash-blossom necklaces that she displayed on the velvet-draped table from his pawn room. Joey Kills the Soldier's mother, after a request translated by Dalah, had supplied a rawhide bag with cedar dust, a gourd and a rattle. Joey's mother had explained that the artifacts were full of religious and symbolic meaning and came from a peyote ceremony.

Abbie stepped back to survey their handiwork with narrowed eyes. They had finished just in time, with the first day of school after the Christmas holidays set to begin in less than thirty minutes.

"It should make the children feel almost like they're in a hogan," Dalah said proudly.

"Maybe we'll see some progress now. I won't have to hold up a couple of fingers and say the word 'two' fifteen times when two eagle feathers explain the concept so much better." Abbie didn't add that maybe she would be able to prevent even one more Indian child from becoming another suicide statistic.

"Your idea was marvelous," Dalah said, shoving her long hair back over her shoulder. She smiled shyly. "I'm glad you asked my help."

Abbie's gaze fell on the beautiful young Indian woman. She liked Dalah very much and yet the thought that perhaps Cody had made love to Dalah was a wrenching knot in the pit of her stomach. She knew that Cody had returned not long after she had, because Orville had happened

—just happened—to mention that Cody had come by the trading post earlier that morning. Astute, perceptive Orville.

What a miserable Christmas they had spent, she and Robert, the boy as miserable and glowering as she. Not even the comic strip wrapped box of candy had elicited a smile from the boy on Christmas morning.

"Mrs. Dennis!"

The name was a bellow. Abbie spun to face the classroom doorway. Miss Halliburton stood there, looking for all the world like a bull about to charge. Her severely tailored gray suit made her look more like a drill sergeant than a school principal. "I have just learned that you took an Indian child off the reservation over the holidays."

What a way to start off the new year! Abbie certainly hoped that this wasn't an omen for the year to come. "I did. But I informed the dormitory."

"Don't you realize, Mrs. Dennis, that any time an Indian child is to be taken off the reservation, it must be cleared with the BIA. That is a governmental offense!"

Abbie drew a deep breath, willing away an angry reaction. "I was unaware of that rule," she said calmly. "It won't happen—"

"What in Beelzebub's name is all this—this paraphernalia?" The principal's index finger jabbed in the direction of the displays.

"Indian artifacts." Abbie saw Dalah's warning

glance but continued smoothly. "I felt that the decorations would make the children feel more at home."

"More at home," the principal purred, and Abbie felt a sudden queasiness in her stomach. "Do you realize the years and time and money we have spent trying to help these children adapt to our culture so that they can make their way in our world? And you—*you*, Mrs. Dennis—without even a by-your-leave from the office—are trying to set our efforts back by a hundred years!"

"I only wanted to—"

Miss Halliburton began to quake visibly. Her face became as ashen as her pewter gray wig. Her voice was a mere rasp. "Is this—is this," she asked, pointing to the rawhide bag of cedar dust, "what I think it is?"

Abbie lost all patience. "I don't know what you think it is, Miss Halliburton."

The principal folded her arms and jutted her head forward. "Am I correct in assuming that this is a peyote ceremonial bag?"

Abbie could see the trouble coming. Clearly the new year was going to be a disastrous one. "Yes."

"Peyote!" It was a roar now. "By all that's holy, Mrs. Dennis! Next you'll even have the peyote buds on display here for the children. Children! How could you?"

There was no point in backing down now. "I did think about displaying peyote buds. But I didn't know where to find them, Miss Halliburton."

The principal clapped her hand across her forehead and leaned against the display table. After a moment she said in a deadly quiet voice, "Get rid of this—this trash, immediately." She turned to leave, then said, "And, Mrs. Dennis, I can assure you that this will go on your record at the BIA headquarters."

"There's no hope of redeeming myself now," Abbie lamented. "That last fiasco with the peyote artifacts really set Miss Halliburton off on a rampage."

Marshall dumped a packet of powdered cream into his coffee. He had gotten into the comfortable habit of having coffee with her in the teacher's lounge every week when he came by for the teachers' order forms. "I'll look into the matter, Abbie. But I can't promise much, since headquarters has jurisdiction over my agency."

She bit her bottom lip. "Marshall . . ." Her voice was almost inaudible. "I can't fail here. I have nowhere else left to go."

His hand covered hers. "You know that you have a place with me. No, I mean it. In every sense of the word. I would ask you to marry me today—except I know that marriage is the last thing you want now."

She managed a small smile and squeezed his strong fingers. "Your offer tempts me. I know I would find a warm, comfortable life with you. But I won't find Abbie Dennis. If I find her anywhere, it will be here at Kaibeto."

No, neither marriage nor men were for her. So

why was it that her thoughts continually turned to Cody? She told herself that it was pointless to see him again, but found herself looking for him every time she went to the trading post.

Even when she closed her eyes at night, in the dark silence of her bedroom, she saw him—the powerful features of his face; the firm, hard curve of his buttocks. She tasted once more his salty flesh, she felt the wiry hair that snaked from his navel downward and she smelled all over again that scent that was uniquely him and affected her like an aphrodisiac.

Thus it was like a blow to her stomach when Linda McNabb, her green eyes wide with awe, showed her the *Phoenix Gazette* toward the end of January. She, Linda, Dorothy and Becky were all relaxing at recess in the teacher's lounge.

Linda flipped down the pages of the society section to locate the article. "There," she said, poking at the photo of a young woman with a gamin haircut and large, heavily fringed eyes behind fashionable rimless glasses. While she wasn't really pretty, there was something very seductive about her. But it was the man standing next to her in the photo whom Linda was pointing at. "Isn't that the Indian artist who lives here at Kaibeto?"

ARIZONA AUTHORESS IN PHOENIX FOR MOVIE PREMIERE. Abbie skipped over the headline to read the text.

Emily DuMonde, who achieved instant success with her first novel, *Ashes of the*

> *Phoenix,* is here for Friday night's gala
> premiere of its screen adaptation. Escort-
> ing her is Arizona's renowned jewelry
> craftsman, Cody Strawhand. Both are
> alumni of Arizona State University.

Becky leaned over Abbie's shoulder. "Holy
Moses, but ain't he a stud!"

"Becky!" Dorothy reproved, but she leaned
closer to get a better look at the photo.

Cody, towering over the authoress, looked very
elegant in a black tuxedo that made his collar-
length hair seem almost as dark. Yet even with his
sophisticated clothing there was still something in
his expression that warned that he was not one of
civilization's tame animals.

Briskly Abbie folded the newspaper and handed it back to Linda. "Studs are a dime a dozen
these days, Becky. You're worldly wise enough to
know that."

"If they were a dime a dozen, you can bet I
wouldn't be teaching in this prison!"

> The man, one of the last of a wild
> breed, looked over the assembly gath-
> ered before him. Dignitaries, the state's
> most powerful businessmen, the press.
> All had come to do him homage. A
> cynical smile curved his lips.

Abbie bent the page's corner and slapped
the book down on the nightstand. So Emily
DuMonde could write. Write well. So what? She

flicked off the lamp. She had better things to do
with her time than stay up until three in the
morning reading. Things like sleeping.

She punched her pillow and turned on her left
side—and went rigid as she heard the front door
knob grate, as if someone were twisting it. It was
a shock because she had come to learn that
Indians simply didn't steal on the reservation. At
least, not sober Indians. But the muffled shout of
"Open the door!" told her that this was a drunk
Indian. Cody.

The peau de soie nightgown swished about her
ankles as she made her way to the living room.
She switched on the front porch light and looked
out the strip of window that ran from floor to
ceiling, the one concession to architectural light-
ness in the subsidized apartment developments.
Cody stood there, his plaid shirt unbuttoned to
his concho-belt. He held a fifth of scotch. Above
his hollowed cheeks his dark eyes were piercing.
"Open up, Abbie, or I'll open the door for you."

"You'll wake the neighbors," she said as loudly
as she dared. "Go away."

"If you don't open it, I'll wake every teacher in
the apartments. Do you want that?"

She bit her lower lip. She had no choice. "All
right," she said, opening the door. "But you can
only stay a minute."

His hand locked on the one with which she still
clasped the doorknob. He loomed over her, his
eyes glittering in the darkness. His warm breath
fanned her face, and the faint scent of whiskey
enveloped her, intoxicating her. He pushed the

door closed and backed her against it. Nervously she pushed away the hair that had fallen over one temple. "What do you want?" she asked, shamming a poise that had deserted her the minute he touched her.

What did he want? How could she ask that? he wondered. He wanted her. He wanted her warmth, her generosity of soul, her strong spirit that was like a candle flame—a glow that lit his darkness, as only she could. He wanted her any way he could have her, but he wanted her forever.

His hands came up to cup her bare shoulders. "You tell me you don't want a commitment," he said in a voice that rasped with the whiskey he had consumed, hoping to drown his need of her. "But you want me. And I'm here to see that you don't go without."

Her heart pounded in her ears like a pneumatic drill. "Not like this," she whispered. "Not coming like a thief in the night . . . not—"

His mouth crushed down on hers, and her hands came up to push against his chest. "Don't!" he mumbled against her lips, and subjugated her mouth with his again.

Resisting his strength was pointless anyway. She remained standing passively within the shackle of his arms. Or tried to. But the narcotic smell of the alcohol on his breath, his tongue mating with her tongue, his lips molded against hers— they all had their effect in weakening her resistance. His hands moved down to cup her buttocks and grind her against him. While he was still kissing her, his fingers worked the slinky nightgown up to her hips and slipped beneath her panties to sensuously knead her flesh.

She angled her chin to better answer his kiss. She could hear herself breathing hard and hated her weakness. Yet her hands, caught against his chest, slid inside the open shirt and searched to find the tiny nipples hidden within the nests of curling hair. Her fingernails flicked them to a button hardness.

He groaned. "I'm going to make love to you, Abbie."

She twisted her mouth free from the domination of his kiss. "No!"

He easily scooped her up against him. "Which way is your bed?"

"Cody, I won't let you do this."

He started walking. "Why not? You admit you want me."

She gasped, but his kiss quieted her protests. His knee found the bed, and he unceremoniously dropped her on the mattress. He stripped his shirt away and kicked off his boots and jeans. She should have moved, but the dim blur of his powerful body transfixed her.

As if he possessed the night vision of a cat, he unerringly reached across the bed to grab one of her ankles and pulled her to the bed's center.

"You wouldn't!" she whispered.

He laughed. "I shouldn't."

Why was she fighting him when she did want him? Slowly, while he watched, her hands inched her lacy bikinis down over legs that she had just

that night shaved and lavished with scented cream
—for him?

When the bikinis dropped to the floor, his
hands captured her ankles and spread them wide.
Sinuously he slid up over her thighs and stomach,
like a giant python that would crush her within its
embrace. He caught her hands and anchored
them above her against the headboard. "Abbie
. . . Abbie . . . your name plays over and over
in my brain like some shaman's ritualistic litany."

To her he was a shaman—a shaman who had
spread his magical medicine like a net over her, a
net she tried one last time to resist. "Cody,
please—let me think. People just don't—"

Gently he kissed each eyelid and pushed the
hair off her forehead. "Abbie . . . I wouldn't
ever want to hurt you. . . . The choice is yours."

She should have been furious, but her imprisoned position only excited her. Above her his eyes
glowed with the same arousal that coursed
through her. She tilted her chin, offering him her
lips. "Cody . . ."

The sound of his name on her lips was enough.
He took her then with the same fierceness of that
first kiss the day of the flash flood. He swore as he
shared the powerful essence of his life with her
that he would make her his physically . . . and
one day he would make her his completely.

Her hand groped in the dark on the nightstand
for a package of cigarettes. And then she remembered again that she had given up smoking. Blast.

She rose up on one elbow and tried to read the digital clock. Almost six. How long had she drifted in that world of semisleep? Beside her Cody's breathing was even. One of his heavy-muscled thighs anchored her calf to the mattress. Her gaze strayed to the fork of his legs, and she had the urge to stroke them, to bring him once again to the state of blinding excitement in which they had met so often during the night.

Another first for her . . . the aggressive love-making she had displayed. At his urging she had become the aggressor, rising above him to take him within her and lead him with her on her wild, exultant ride until she collapsed, her hair tumbling across his face and shoulders. Afterward, he had stroked her hair, whispering words of praise for his warrioress.

He had talked later—in his sleep—and tossed, pushing the sheets from his sweat-soaked body. He had mumbled about a suicide—a showerhead —Indian children caught between two worlds. And she knew what for her was a tragedy was for him a living nightmare.

She knew that she was falling in love with him. He wasn't an ordinary man. He was stimulating to be with. The quiet, forceful way he spoke, the intent way he listened, the thorough way he made love—gentle yet resourceful. Why couldn't they have met years ago? He was a man whom she wanted to be with, . . . but could she tie herself to him forever?

Careful not to shift the mattress, she blindly felt about on the floor for her gown and retrieved it.

Stealthily she edged her leg from beneath his. But when she went to rise, his hand entwined in her long hair, forcing her head back.

"You're still running away, aren't you?"

"I've got to get ready for school."

He released her hair and rolled to a sitting position, his arm propped on one crooked knee. "You know what I mean, Abbie."

She sprang from the bed, the gown held protectively in front of her. "What do you want from me?" she asked. He said nothing but regarded her with such a piercing look that she cried out, "I can't, Cody! Don't you understand? I'm not Spartan like you. I can't be content with——"

—living like an Indian? Instead she finished, "I want more from life than you do."

"You're a coward."

"No more than you. At least I don't hide out from the world. Walking on the perimeters of society, afraid to get involved. At least I'm trying to find my place."

"And what is your place? Are you nothing but a pretentious socialite who takes but cannot give?"

"Damn it!" she cried. "That's all I've done is give, give and give and give." Her fists clenched at her sides; the gown slithered down about her ankles. Tears spiked her lashes. "It's my turn now!"

"Giving and taking can't be done by turns."

"You ought to know—I'd be willing to bet that Emily DuMonde does a lot of giving."

He arched one brow. His smile when it came

was scintillating. "Perhaps she's more of a woman than you are."

Her hand arced back to slap him. "Don't try it," he ordered. "I'll only end up making love to you again."

"You don't know what making love is!"

"And you do?"

His thrust hit home, pierced through to her core. "Get out!"

In one fluid movement Cody rose from the bed and scooped up his jeans. Proudly unashamed of his nakedness, he stood before her and snapped them on. "I'm finished trying to find the real Abbie Dennis." He tossed his shirt over one shoulder. He paused at the bedroom door. "When you find her, let me know."

This time Abbie was careful to obtain permission for the Flagstaff field trip from the BIA in Gallop through the principal's office. Without being told, she knew that she was on parole, that it would take just one more incident, even a minor one, and she would be denied the opportunity to renew the final year's portion of her two-year contract.

"And just how do you propose to finance such an outing?" the principal demanded.

"Remember the beads the children made? We had them sold in Tuba City."

Miss Halliburton drummed her pen against the desk. "Did you look into all the ramifications of such—"

"I took care of everything," Abbie hastened to

reassure her, fearing that the older woman would refuse permission for the field trip.

"Frankly, the best thing that could happen for everyone around here would be for you to quit, Mrs. Dennis."

"But I won't."

Miss Halliburton looked down her romanesque nose at Abbie. "I'm beginning to realize that that's one of your most noticeable characteristics —indomitability. A dangerous thing."

"And you wouldn't say that you also share that trait, Miss Halliburton?"

The principal's eyes narrowed. "Yes. But I was intelligent enough—or perhaps I should say humble enough—not to come out to Kaibeto trying to change things to my way of thinking. It just so happens that the teachers who came before us might have known something more than we do."

Forgoing the issue, Abbie reverted to the original subject. "The sale of the necklaces raised enough money for the field trip. If I can find enough teachers and aides to volunteer to supervise the children . . ."

"And what about transportation?"

"I thought I would see if we could borrow the Red Lake Boarding School's two buses. We could make it to Flagstaff and back in one day."

"You realize that I'm almost hoping something goes awry?"

"Yes."

Dear Lord, please don't let Robert run off again, Abbie prayed.

She considered leaving the boy behind, but

rejected the idea. He would probably choose just that time to run away from the school. Why had she had to end up with Robert? Ever since his father had failed to show up at Christmas, the boy had refused to participate in class. No longer would he even draw his pictures of Navajo Mountain. He simply stared out the window at February's denuded trees and bleak, barren landscape. Why couldn't he have picked on another teacher?

She would just have to keep a hawk's eye on him, which didn't present that much difficulty in the end. The boy sat stolidly in the bus while the other children squealed and bounced and touched everything with curious fingers. Dalah and Becky, who hoped to see her lumberjack, had volunteered to help patrol the children. Even Marshall, when Miss Halliburton submitted Abbie's proposed itinerary to his office, had elected to go along.

Abbie, Becky, Dalah, Marshall—it seemed that they laughed with true enjoyment for the entire trip. They laughed at the Flagstaff Depot, when the train whistled in and the children hid their faces from the fire-breathing monster; they laughed at the supermarket, where the children made faces in the mirror over the vegetable bins; they even laughed on the paved streets, where the concrete gutters banked the curbs and the children got down on their knees, looking to see how deep the drainage holes were and yelling in to hear their echoes.

"I can't remember when I've had so much fun," Marshall said on the return trip.

Dalah sat on the seat next to him, wiping the tears of laughter from her cheeks. Abbie, who sat with Becky across the aisle from Dalah and Marshall, caught the way the young Indian girl watched Marshall as he talked, and something in Dalah's gaze made Abbie wonder. Could it possibly be Marshall whom Dalah cared for?

Despite the merriment, Abbie returned from the excursion worn out and feeling lousy. Aspirin wasn't the answer, and she made her way to the trading post just before closing time. "I don't know what it is," she told Orville, "but being corralled with thirty-four screaming children on a bus would drive even a saint to drink."

"I've got just the thing," Orville assured her and groped beneath the counter. "Left over from our last bout at Cody's house."

"Oh, no. A drink right now would wrap my intestines in a Gordian knot."

Besides, just the mention of Cody's name reminded her of that first night she had spent with him at his house—that was when her troubles had really started. That was when she had become preoccupied with Cody Strawhand to the exclusion of all else. The way he looked at her; the way he touched her. Brad had never made her feel like Cody did. Cody made her feel like a complete woman. Like the *kachina* doll when it was finally painted.

She tried to tell herself that she was merely reliving her high school infatuation days all over again. Still, the bottom of her stomach felt like it dropped out when, at the next moment, the bell

tingled on the trading post door and Cody walked
in. He seemed to fill the dim room, large though it
was. His father had that same presence, a charisma that had taken Chase Strawhand all the way to
the governor's mansion in Santa Fe.

Cody's eyes foraged over her, taking in the
suede sheath that hugged her svelte figure; then it
was as though he looked right through her, as if
she weren't even there. It was a terrible feeling,
being reduced to insignificance. Never had that
happened to her.

A weathered old Indian woman in a calico
blouse and a brilliant turquoise satin skirt lined up
at the counter behind Abbie, and Abbie was
forced to pay for the box of extrastrength pain-
relief tablets. She could play it cool, too. When
she passed by Cody, she inclined her head in a
regal manner that would have been the envy of a
White House receiving line. For one frightening
second she thought that he wasn't going to let her
pass.

Cody smiled sardonically. He could bed a hundred women, he thought with disgust, and still he
would see Abbie's face imprinted over theirs.

He knew that she wouldn't stay at Kaibeto, that
the boarding school was a temporary catharsis for
her. She couldn't take reservation life any more
than his mother had been able to. At year's end
she would walk out.

But where to? Marshall? He doubted it, because that would keep her on the reservation.
Cody knew that the BIA's Western director came
over every week specifically to see Abbie, and it

had become all Cody could do to maintain the appearance of the friendship he had shared with Marshall. Marshall was one of the few Anglo men he admired, an honest man who truly cared about the welfare of the Indians. It wasn't just a job for Marshall, though it might have started out that way. But Marshall's good points didn't lessen the sudden cooling he felt for the man.

No, Cody thought. He couldn't make that same mistake his father had made and try to make a socialite his. Abbie was too much like his own mother. Besides, she would only want to change him, to remake him into a successful capitalist like her former husband. If she had her way, he'd no doubt end up wheeling and dealing out of Cambria.

They had no future together, and he would have to make a point of remembering that.

Chapter 9

"Now, THIS," ABBIE SAID, JABBING THE UMBRELla's handle into the large inverted cardboard box that Orville had provided, "is our television."

She hadn't foreseen any problems in her students trying to read a simple primer. Everything had gone well until the children in one story had decided to watch television. The Indian children hadn't the faintest idea what a television set was. Why hadn't she thought of taking them into a department store when they were in Flagstaff to look at television sets?

At the one department store that they had visited, the children had been astounded that so much clothing existed, when for them one change of clothing was sufficient. It made sense to Abbie.

Just as the nearly circular hogans made better sense than the white man's square houses—you never had to sweep out the difficult-to-reach corners when there simply weren't any corners.

She must really be losing touch with reality, when a dirt-floor hogan is beginning to seem preferable to the electrical conveniences of a multiroom estate in Philadelphia, Abbie thought. Conveniences? The task of keeping those electrical appliances in working order had often made them more of an encumbrance than a convenience.

But the thought of Philadelphia brought a pang of homesickness for her boys. They had written with a promise to vacation in Arizona over the summer, but summer seemed so far off, still three months away. It was the homesickness, she told herself, that made her feel weepy lately, a condition so totally alien to her. For so long it had seemed that she had forgotten how to cry . . . until that day in the old mill house when Cody had taught her what sexual fulfillment really was.

"Children," she said abruptly, "recess." She really must get out of her doldrums. Along with the children, who jerked their coats from their pegs, she slid into her own coat and went out to brave the brisk weather.

Becky joined her. The girl sat on the school steps, flipping through a magazine and puffing on a cigarette as if she were sending out smoke signals. Abbie fanned away the billowing cigarette smoke that churned her stomach.

Becky looked up through a curtain of lanky hair. "Gee, Mrs. Dennis, you really look green."

"I can't imagine why, Becky."

Abbie took a seat one step lower than the young teacher so that the smoke drifted up and away from her. Out of habit, her gaze swept over the playground full of laughing children. Like the Navajo woman who, without counting her hundred-odd sheep, knows instantly if one is missing, Abbie had reached the point when she knew immediately if a child was absent. Yes, beneath the willow—apart from the other children—stood Robert, his eyes like obsidian stones.

He was thinner than he had been, but what worried Abbie most was that he had resumed his habit of staring at Navajo Mountain. She knew that he was once again contemplating running away. It mattered little that he invariably went to Cody's. If he left just once more, and if Miss Halliburton found out, that was all it would take to jeopardize her job.

Oh, dear God, she prayed, let his father come at Easter break. The thought of Robert taking off again was enough to make her stomach roll, which it seemed to be doing often lately.

Two weeks later, as she fried bacon early one morning before school, the reason for her unsettled stomach came to her when she rushed to the sink and hung her head over the drain. She grabbed the dish towel off the refrigerator door handle and soaked the terrycloth under cool water. Holding the towel to her perspiration-sheened face, she began to cry in great shuddering spasms.

No, no, no . . . not at her age . . . it wasn't fair. All those years when she had wanted so badly to conceive . . . and now . . . What a naive little idiot she had been.

She braced her hands against the counter and tried to tell herself that she could be wrong. After all, she had never been that regular. And her nausea? She could attribute it to the great strain she had been under lately. The hectic days when she worried about her contract being terminated; the sleepless nights when she tossed about trying to shake the image of Cody's supple bronze hands making love to her again—or worse, to someone else.

Oh, damn him!

She would simply make an appointment with a doctor in Flagstaff and settle the question once and for all. Getting there presented more of a problem. Becky and her lumberjack had quarreled, and she was no longer seeing him. Abbie hated to ask Marshall to drive her all the way into Flagstaff, but she saw no alternative.

She asked him Thursday when he came to have coffee with her, explaining that she needed to see the doctor about an allergy problem that had only cropped up since she had moved to Arizona. He was more than happy to oblige. "I'll pick you up Saturday, Abbie, and we can make a day of it."

Saturday morning she was running late, as was

becoming habitual with her lately. It seemed to
take so long to get her stomach settled. She
required three cups of coffee—and some toast,
but nothing more—before she could operate effi-
ciently. Marshall's knock at the door caught her
only partially dressed.

"Come on in," she called out.

The door opened and shut, and she said, "Back
here, Marshall. I've got a stuck zipper. Here, see
if you can budge it."

She lifted her heavy hair over one arm and
walked to the bedroom door to meet him—and
came face to face with Cody. Her lips parted in
shock. For one naked moment they stood looking
at each other, separated only by inches, close
enough for her to see the fine wrinkles carved by
time and weather that fanned about his sulphur-
ous eyes.

"Turn around," he said.

Slowly she pivoted, still holding the cascade of
her hair over her forearm to display the cinnamon
velour dress that hung open to expose her spine.
"Why are you here?" Her voice sounded breathless even to her own ears.

"Marshall telephoned this morning." His fingers closed over the zipper, brushing tantalizingly
against the small of her back. "The BIA called
their directors into Gallop at the last minute for a
seminar. He asked me if I could—"

"I know—you're to be my transportation
again." Her eyes closed and she stifled a groan.
Why did *everything* have to go wrong?

The zipper paused midway up her back. "You're not wearing a bra," he said in a voice that seemed ominously quiet.

If he so much as touched her, she knew that all her self-control would shatter. "The snap broke— and I didn't have time to search for another." How could she explain that her breasts felt so full and tender that a binding bra was acutely uncomfortable?

He finished zipping the dress and hooked the bateau neckline. "Let's go," he said harshly.

She was even more uncomfortable during the long drive into Flagstaff. A tense silence vibrated between them. If she got sick while she was with Cody . . . Oh, no. "May I have a cigarette, please?"

He flicked her a scrutinizing glance. "When did you take up smoking again?"

"I . . . uh . . ." Really, she should be able to handle this situation, delicate though it was, in an adult manner. "Nerves, I suppose."

He withdrew a cigarette package from his shirt pocket and shook one out for her. "Is that why you're seeing a doctor?"

Her eyes flew up to his, then lowered as she held the cigarette to his proffered lighter, a silver case inlaid with turquoise. "Yes."

A spiral of smoke drifted up from between her lips. "About that night at my apartment," she began edgily, "I—I won't try to deny that you— that I've enjoyed your lovemaking as I never did with my husband, but . . ."

"But—" he drawled with a reckless slant to his lips, "another man might serve your needs just as well. Like Marshall, maybe."

"That's unfair!"

"But true, isn't it? As long as you don't have to form any kind of long-term relationship."

She stabbed the cigarette out in the ashtray. "This conversation is getting us nowhere."

"Which is just as well with me. Because making love to you is like being nowhere. Any woman would be as good, Abbie, maybe better."

Her sharply indrawn breath seared her lungs. The words stung. What she had experienced with him had been special to her, but obviously not for him, when he had women queued up before his door like actresses at an audition. "I'm sorry that I ever—that—"

"That you ever made love to *me,* an Indian?" he taunted.

She smiled coolly. "I'm sorry that I put out that cigarette. I'd like another."

She could only be thankful that the doctor she had chosen was a family practitioner. Several of the patients, men and women both, glanced up curiously when she and Cody entered the waiting room. "A golden Anglo woman with a brown-skinned Indian," Cody mocked at her ear. "I'm sure the patients will all have something to tell their family and friends this afternoon."

"You're about as Indian as I am," she muttered, and snapped open a magazine.

Cody chose to annoy her. His arm encircled her shoulder, as if she were indeed his wife, his fingers etching imaginary circles on her upper arm. "Your magazine is upside down, Abbie."

She shook her shoulders. "Stop it."

"What?"

"What you're doing."

"I didn't know I was doing anything."

She glared up into his lambent eyes. Unreasonably, she felt like crying again. She did cry an hour later when the doctor finished his examination.

"Yes, I'm certain, Mrs. Dennis. You're pregnant, though still in the early stages. Maybe two months. I would say you're due around the end of August. There, now," he said, placing a kindly hand on her shoulder. "Don't cry about it. A lot of women start second families at your age. Thirty-seven's still young enough to adjust to such a situation."

Strangely enough, the news made her stronger. Maybe Miss Halliburton had been right about her indomitability. When she was at the bottom, it seemed that she fought back best.

A cold mantle of logic settled over her on the return trip to Kaibeto. The idea of not having the baby never entered her mind. That alternative was too high an emotional price for her to live with. She would simply have the baby and return to teaching in September. Linda McNabb had done it at another Indian boarding school. There was no reason why she couldn't do it, too. Of course, there would be Miss Halliburton to contend with.

What concerned her more was Cody's finding

out. She wanted nothing that would bind her to him or any man again. But what would he do when her pregnancy became obvious? She glanced at his dark profile against the evening sunset. He would be perceptive enough to come to the right conclusion. He had known by her initial and apprehensive reticence at his lovemaking, followed by her deep emotional reaction, that there hadn't been any other man in her life since she had left Brad.

And she sensed that, once he made up his mind, he would not easily give up what he considered his.

She would just have to make certain that he would be unsure who the baby's father was. She opened the pickup door and said sweetly over her shoulder, "Tell Marshall I'm sorry I missed him."

The nausea had finally subsided; when Abbie glanced in the mirror she saw a striking champagne blonde with iridescent blue eyes and a glowing complexion. She seemed to shimmer with that mysterious and scintillating essence that women pay a fortune for in creams and beauty foods and health salons. She smoothed the sweater dress of ecru flaxspun over her still taut stomach and let out a sigh of thanksgiving. Her secret was safe for the time being, though she had yet to face the Dragon Lady.

Although it was the end of March, spring whispered of its imminent arrival in the brisk, nippy wind. It was an almost perfect day for the

Easter egg hunt before spring vacation began, yet she lamented the fact that the landscape had about as much grass as her living room floor.

In the classroom the children chattered incessantly, eager to begin the hunt, a novelty for them. For three weeks they had worked on their Easter baskets, made out of shoeboxes. Karen Many Goats won for the best-looking basket; hers looked like a rabbit, with its coat-hanger ears covered in fluffy cotton balls. Leo Her Many Horses won for the best-decorated egg, painted to look like an ear of corn. Robert, naturally, had refused to make a basket or paint an egg at all.

Abbie had mixed emotions about the egg hunt. All the teachers had enthusiastically contributed their time to the project. Some teachers pitched in at the cafeteria to boil the hundreds of eggs, others colored them, and still others painted names and designs. But when Becky had volunteered to hide them while the other teachers corralled the rambunctious students, Abbie had had no idea that the younger woman would run into Cody at the trading post and ask for his help.

Abbie hadn't seen him since the day he had driven her into Flagstaff, and she dreaded this face-to-face meeting. Somehow she felt as if her secret were printed on her forehead with scarlet letters. The worst was that she continued to think about him during the day—unconsciously doodling his name—and to dream erotic fantasies about him at night.

It did little good to tell herself that Cody

Strawhand was a lone wolf, that he was as contemptuous of her high society breeding as she was of his nonconformity. The image of his body posed over hers—and other images that crimsoned her skin—ate away at her like a cancer. She had always thought that she was ready to face any challenge, but she was afraid to meet Cody again, afraid of the sensual weakness she had discovered within herself.

Any hope that Becky had cherished of making eyes at Cody was crushed when, on the morning of the hunt, Miss Halliburton posted herself next to him. And any hope that Abbie had entertained of avoiding the man was extinguished. His gaze riveted her where she stood with her students.

When Miss Halliburton asked him something, his gaze released Abbie from her paralysis. She forced herself to calmly approach the two. Cody was pointing out to the principal the perimeters within which he had hidden the eggs. The spring wind had picked up, whipping Cody's mane of hair, bound though it was by the bandana, across his chiseled face. It was all Abbie could do to hold down the hem of her dress that danced dangerously high about her thighs. His gaze ran up and down the length of her legs. She didn't miss the provoking grin he flashed at her predicament.

"I would offer to help . . ." he challenged.

Miss Halliburton raised a censorious brow. "Mr. Strawhand!"

"My apologies." But his eyes laughed at Abbie. She had read something somewhere about the laughing eyes of the Navajo, and now she understood. His laughter was infectious; it was all she could do to keep a straight face.

Then suddenly his eyes narrowed in sharp scrutiny. His gaze scanned her face in an unnerving fashion before dropping to peruse her breasts in such an intimate manner that she blushed. He couldn't possibly know. No, she was just becoming paranoid.

Still, she swung away to join the other teachers, who were already herding their charges out onto the far-reaching stretches of red sand sparsely splotched with wretched clumps of desert grass. Miss Halliburton and Cody followed closely enough that she could hear his deep, rich voice. "Since there was no place to hide the eggs," he was telling the principal, "I buried them with my boot heel so that just a little of the paint shows."

The Easter egg hunt was like nothing Abbie had ever seen. She had expected a wild stampede when Miss Halliburton gave the signal. Incredibly, the children fanned out in a line as straight as a cavalry flank and slowly moved forward. Their eyes, the observant eyes of the true marksman, swept over the ground before them. Their sight homed in more accurately than any metal detector. Even more surprising was the way the children retrieved their booty—not all rushing to pick up the discovered egg but letting the child directly in its path collect it.

Following the students, Cody walked alongside Abbie and the stern-faced Miss Halliburton and

joked every so often in Navajo with the children.
Then it happened. That horrible moment when
the wind swept Miss Halliburton's wig from her
head. "Oh, no!" she yelled in anguish. Her hands
flew up to cover a head that was sparsely covered
with short, brittle hairs. More scalp than hair was
exposed.

The children—the teachers—Cody and Abbie
—all stopped and turned to stare in confusion at
the phenomenon of an almost-bald woman, while
the wig hurtled past them. The principal glanced
desperately about her. "Oh, get it!" she cried out
when nobody moved. "Oh, please, help me!"
Tears of shame spilled over her veined hands. The
nearest to her, Delbert and Joey, took out after
the bouncing ball of hair, but sprint though they
might, the wind blew the wig just ahead of their
short legs.

"It's all right, Miss Halliburton," Abbie said,
touching the woman's arm in a consoling gesture.

Then Cody did something utterly unexpected.
He unknotted the bandana from about his forehead and, covering the woman's naked head, tied
it under her quivering chin.

Abbie saw the look of deep gratitude Miss
Halliburton bestowed on Cody. The woman's
trembling hands wiped the tears that furrowed
her powdered cheeks. She leaned her head into
his shoulder. "When I was a child—scarlet
fever—" she hiccoughed. "The illness—it took all
my hair. No man could ever want me."

Abbie stood openmouthed. The dragon had
changed into a kitten.

"I bet you never gave any man half a chance, did you, Miss Halliburton?" Cody said gently.

The woman sniffed into his shirt. "I was too afraid . . ."

"Of rejection," he finished for her. Over her head his gaze met Abbie's, and she read the challenge in his eyes.

Deliberately she looked down just as Delbert ran up with the wig clutched in his hand. When she looked up again, Cody was leading Miss Halliburton, her wig now safely in hand, back to her office.

Damn him! Little children and old ladies. He should have been a Boy Scout.

Her purse under one arm, a stack of papers that she had meant to grade over the Easter vacation in the other, Abbie shoved her apartment door open with her hip. As she should have expected, the sheaf of papers slid onto the floor, the homework scattering like blown leaves.

"Hell," she muttered and went down on all fours to collect them.

It had been a record day for testing the validity of the Peter Principle. Everything that could have gone wrong, did. First, Cody showing up for the Easter Egg hunt, as if his prime purpose was to annoy her. Then Miss Halliburton's wig blowing away. For the rest of the day the woman had made St. George's dragon seem tame.

But the worst had been when Robert's father hadn't come for him at the end of the day, when Easter vacation began. She had watched helpless⌐

ly as the boy, hands jammed in his jean pockets,
his foot kicking at random rocks, made his way
back to the dormitory. Before she left for the
week, she had stopped by the dormitory to warn
Dalah to keep a close watch on Robert. That was
all she needed now, for the boy to take flight.

The one bright spot in the day had been Marshall's visit—and his invitation. The Easter vacation had looked like seven long, boring days at
Kaibeto, but Marshall's invitation for a three-day
spree in Las Vegas had been like a visit from one's
guardian angel or an IRS refund—unexpected but
desperately needed. Her slightly hesitant response had prompted Marshall to add wryly, "No
strings attached, Abbie. Only the pleasure of
your company."

But it wasn't merely the lure of a pleasant way
to spend the Easter holidays that had prompted
her to accept; if word got back that she had spent
three days in Las Vegas with Marshall—yes, that
could be the solution to her problem.

Scooping up several more wayward sheets,
Abbie had to smile smugly at how adroitly she
was working out what had threatened to be a
sticky situation . . . until her eyes encountered
the scuffed boot before her. Slowly, reluctantly,
her gaze followed the jeans leg upward. There
Cody sat on her sofa, arms spread across its back,
one ankle propped on the other knee.

"How . . . how did you get in here?" she asked
in a low voice.

His smile didn't quite reach his eyes. "Oh, we

Indians have devious methods of breaking and entering."

She pushed herself up on her knees and shoved a swath of hair back off her forehead. "Now that you've entered, you can just leave."

He leaned forward and she almost jumped, she was so edgy. Calmly he clasped his hands between his knees. "I will when I find out the answer to my question."

"Try the school. I've finished answering questions for the day."

"This isn't a student's question."

She came to her feet and turned away. "I only get paid to answer students' questions," she flipped over her shoulder with a nonchalance she was far from feeling, and continued into the kitchen. "Now, would you please leave?"

In three strides he was across the room. Jerking her around by her arm to face him, he cornered her against the counter. His eyes blistered hers. "I want to know the answer—now."

Tomorrow, she promised herself, she was going to buy five cartons of cigarettes. "And what will you do if I refuse to answer you—seduce me like you did the last time you showed up at my apartment?"

His voice was unnaturally soft. One hand came up to caress the angle of her jaw. "I would hardly call that seduction, my love." She tried to avert her face, but his fingers held her jaw firmly. "That was total unconditional surrender on your part."

Her lids drooped before those penetrating eyes.

"You've got your history mixed up. It was the Indians who surrendered, and surrendered and surrendered."

"And you're forgetting Custer's fate. Now, are you going to tell me what I want to know?"

She forced her eyes to meet his unflinchingly, forced the firmness into her voice that she would have used with one of her recalcitrant students. "Cody, whatever happened between us didn't work out. But there's no reason why we can't establish some sort of friendship."

He released her jaw then, but blocked any avenue of escape by locking his hands on the counter's edge to either side of her waist. "Yes, there is Abbie. What's between us is too powerful to contain in some mild-mannered friendship. It's either everything or nothing."

"Well, then, I choose the latter."

"You're not the only party involved in this relationship. And I mean for it to be the former."

Her eyes flashed up into his. "And just how do you propose to achieve this feat?"

He lifted a brow. "Didn't you know that Indians are relentless?"

"And has Miss Halliburton told you yet that my one vice is indomitability?"

"When two equal forces collide . . ." He grunted. "Abbie, I'm finished bantering words around with—"

"—with someone who speaks with a forked tongue?" she asked archly.

"Damn it, Abbie." He grabbed her shoulders and shook her. "You're pregnant, aren't you?"

"No!" she gasped out.

"Don't lie to me. I know your body as intimately as any doctor or your husband ever did. Your breasts—they're fuller. Your complexion—you practically glow with sudden robust health."

She pushed aside his arm. It would be fruitless to deny the pregnancy. He would find out soon enough, when she had to resort to maternity dresses. "Yes, I am." She moved past him to stand in front of the vertical window next to the door.

"But what happened between you and me," she continued in a toneless voice, "does not give you any right to interrogate me."

"It does when you're carrying my child," he rasped out behind her.

If ever she was to escape, to be her own woman . . . Slowly she turned to face him. He watched her with the intensity of an Old West tracker. She would have to be convincing. "When? How about 'if,' Cody?"

The light in the room was growing dim, and his eyes glinted with the incandescence of some night creature's. His voice, when he spoke, was measured. "I don't like guessing games. What exactly are you implying?"

She drew a deep, fortifying breath. "Cody, I hate to damage your supreme masculine ego, but you're not the only man I have been seeing."

He crossed the intervening space to stand before her. His hands cupped either side of her head. "You may be seeing Marshall," he said quietly, "but I would know if you have given yourself to him. And you haven't."

She played her last card. "That's merely your male vanity speaking. How can you be so certain? Why else would I be going off to Las Vegas with him tomorrow for the Easter holidays?"

Chapter 10

WITH ONE OF THOSE UNEXPECTED REVERSALS CHARacteristic of high desert weather, winter howled
back through northern Arizona. The wind blew
across old Flagstaff, down past the railroad tracks
and up Santa Fe Avenue, making the turn-of-the-
century buildings look even more decrepit than
usual, as if they huddled against each other to
shield their worn facades from further aging.

College kids in snow-country clothes and cowboys in heavy sheepskin coats hunkered down by
Pulliam Airport's see-through fireplace, waiting
the next plane out or in, not a regular occurrence
in that airport that looked more like a ranch
house headquarters, with its shingled roof and
native stone facade. Every so often someone
would toss a log on the fire to keep it properly

glowing. A Hopi Indian sat reading a college text on the Continental Congress while his redheaded neighbor absorbed a book on Kiva art.

Abbie, dressed warmly but fashionably in riding boots and a calfskin leather skirt and jacket, plunked several coins into the vending machine and retrieved her package of cigarettes from the tray below. Her nerves were badly frazzled. The confrontation with Cody the previous day had wreaked havoc with her composure. She felt like some medieval tapestry being plundered by a raiding cossack . . . frayed and rent by his angry lance.

Oh, Cody hadn't as much as touched her the day before, when she had announced her planned excursion with Marshall. He had simply stared at her with eyes that scorched her with their loathing, which terrified her more than his few explosions of anger ever had. Then he had coolly swung away from her and left her apartment.

As she tore off the cigarette package's cellophane wrapper, she reminded herself that she had achieved the freedom from Cody that she had sought with relatively little problem. Or so she thought . . . until the turquoise-inlaid lighter appeared with its tongue of flame in front of the cigarette she held between her fingers. She looked up into Cody's dark eyes.

"Where's Marshall?" he asked.

"Parking the car." She tipped her cigarette to the flame and inhaled. Lifting her head, she let the smoke drift slowly from between her lips, then said, "I suppose it's a coincidence that you're here."

"Quite." His eyes laughed, crinkles fanning from their outer edges, but she caught the challenge reflected in their depths. He was dressed in tobacco brown corduroy slacks and a down vest of lambskin. "I'm flying out to L.A. to negotiate an art show."

"You don't expect me to believe that."

He grinned and pocketed the lighter. "I would be surprised if you did—after I warned you how relentless we Indians are."

"Why?" It was a husky whisper.

He leaned back against the airport bulletin board that was covered with notices and flight information and crossed one boot over the other. "After I left you, I started thinking more rationally. Call it male ego, if you wish, but I know you, Abbie. Better than you realize. And I know that the child you carry is mine."

"I told you that—"

He held up a forestalling hand. "And I also know that, even if I weren't the father of the child, I'd still want you."

She felt like screaming right there before everyone. "Don't you understand," she sputtered, "that *I* don't want *you?* I don't want any man! Now go on back to your hogan and your hermit's life."

He grinned. "Sorry. I've already made up my mind to have you. Besides, like I told you, I have to fly out to L.A."

"I just bet!"

"There you are," Marshall called out. Looking extremely handsome in a white ski jacket that enhanced his suntanned face, he crossed to her. "Cody, great to see you!"

"He was just leaving," Abbie said.

"On my way to Los Angeles," Cody explained.

Marshall sighed. "Looks like we might as well be. Sky West just informed me that there's a layover at Page followed by a change of flights in St. George, Utah, before we ever make it to Las Vegas."

Above the high ridges of his cheekbones Cody's eyes glinted, and Abbie knew what was coming. "I pass right over Las Vegas, Marshall. Why don't you let me drop you two off there?"

Marshall arched a questioning brow at Abbie. "It would save us a lot of time."

"And airfare," Cody said. "You can invest a couple of dollars for me on the roulette table."

"Sounds like a good idea," Marshall said.

"We . . . I can't." Abbie looked at Marshall pleadingly. "I get a nervous stomach when I fly in light aircraft."

"That's no problem," Cody said smoothly. "I keep a packet of air sickness tablets in the Cherokee's glove compartment."

"Great!" Marshall said.

"Great," Abbie echoed dully.

So, Cody was flying them to Las Vegas. He wouldn't dare invite himself along.

He would. He did.

The plane was winging low over Hoover Dam, with her in the copilot's seat, when he flicked a leering grin at her. He turned to Marshall in the back seat. "It just happens that I don't have to be in L.A. until the day after tomorrow. You wouldn't mind if I lay over here, would you, Marshall? I'd find something to do with my time while you two are . . . busy. I could take in the shows, sit in a couple of hands of twenty-one. . . ."

"Of course not," Marshall said. "We could even arrange to meet for dinner."

Abbie could think of no objection to raise. Cody's air sickness tablet was having its tranquilizing effect on her, so she could only acquiesce to whatever the predator suggested. And predator he was. He was stalking her as the primitive Indian did the helpless deer.

No, she wasn't completely helpless. She managed to glare at him later while Marshall withdrew their luggage from the baggage compartment at the rear of the Cherokee. "You're taking advantage of Marshall's friendship for you," she accused.

His eyes made love to her lips. "I'm merely making certain I keep what's mine."

"I am not yours!"

Her denial had little effect on Cody. She found herself wedged between him and Marshall on the cab trip into Las Vegas, with Cody's arm across the back of the seat, subtly staking his claim to her. She thought about explaining to Marshall just what Cody was up to, but the story wasn't very pretty. And it could only hurt Marshall. She liked him too much for that.

They checked into the hotel, and Marshall insisted that Cody get a room on the same floor as theirs. "That way we can check in with each other," he said congenially.

If ever Abbie had considered staging an orgy, her hotel room would have served as an excellent location. It had a royal purple velvet spread and window curtains, plush carpeting of lavender blue and, incredibly, mirrored walls—and ceiling. She looked into the mirror and said, "You won't get away with it, Cody Strawhand."

It seemed that he was as obstinate and perverse as she was—and as cunning as Geronimo. He was with Marshall when they met before dinner for drinks at the hotel bar. Abbie never heard the entertainer at the piano. She was too disconcerted by the hand that stroked her knee.

He was with them when they visited the casino. While he and Marshall played several chummy hands of single-deck twenty-one, she desultorily dropped quarters into a one-armed bandit, unwilling to risk more of her teacher's salary. Every so often she glanced at the two men. Cody, with the bandana about his forehead, was every inch the handsome savage and drew frequent visits from the cigarette girl.

He was with them when they took a cab to another hotel to watch a famous comic's act. In the darkened room she was squeezed into the circular booth between him and Marshall. Marshall held her hand—while Cody's fingers idly stroked the back of her neck.

He was with them when they returned to the

casino, where Marshall lost at roulette and Cody won at craps. The two men drank and laughed like bosom buddies, and she watched. She listened to the clicking whir of the ivory ball on the roulette wheel, the incessant ringing of the slot machines, the raucous laughter—and wondered what she was doing there.

He was with them when they returned to their hotel to catch the midnight show. Before curtain time, while Cody engaged Marshall in a lively debate over Indian subsidized housing, she sat and smoked and fumed.

And he was with them when they rode the elevator up to their rooms. By that time, after several screwdrivers, Marshall was feeling too good to give her much more than a merry peck on the cheek and saunter off to his own room, still chuckling over some quip of Cody's.

Abbie felt that Cody had missed his calling; he should have been a recreation director on some cruise ship. She jammed her key into her door. When it didn't give, Cody said affably, "Here, let me help you."

"I don't need your help, thank you."

He unlocked the door easily, but when he pushed it open, she whirled to block his entrance. "Oh, no, Cody Strawhand, you sneaking, conniving excuse for a human being. You may get your way with Marshall, but you won't with me."

He smiled amiably. "It was a miserable way to start off your vacation, wasn't it?"

"You know it was," she gritted.

"You're here to gamble and have fun, Abbie.

Gamble with me"—he shrugged—"and maybe you can have your fun after all."

Her eyes narrowed. "Just what are you suggesting?"

"Can't we sit down and talk about it?"

"No."

He feigned a sigh. "You don't trust me."

"Correct."

"All right, then. What I propose is simple. You choose your game of cards—poker, twenty-one, gin, what have you. If you win, I leave you and Marshall alone."

Her teeth nibbled on her lower lip. "And if I lose?"

"You spend the rest of the week with me."

She was desperate—but not that desperate. "Tell me, Cody," she said sweetly, "doesn't it bother your Indian's sense of honor to do this to your friend?"

He bent his head to kiss her on the ear. "Not when I know Marshall would make a better mate for Dalah."

"But Dalah—she's in love with you, isn't she?"

He chuckled. "Wrong. We're from the same clan, Abbie, and Indians don't marry within the clan. She considers me more a big brother."

Goose bumps broke out where his tongue flicked her neck. "But you can't be sure that she would make a better mate for Marshall."

"She's been in love with him since she was in the ninth grade. And he might have seen her worth had you not come and blinded him with your aristocratic beauty."

"You say that almost as if you hate it—my aristocratic beauty, as you call it."

He straightened and, bracing his hand against the door frame above her head, looked down at her. The amusement, mingled with shrewd determination, that had flickered in the depths of his eyes ever since they had left Pulliam Airport temporarily gave way to solemnity. "I hate exposing myself to the weakness that comes in loving you."

"A weakness?" she asked breathlessly.

"Perhaps I should say pain. Any time someone opens himself up, reveals his innermost feelings, he's exposing himself to the pain of possible rejection." Rejection—it was a word he had learned as a child. Was he being foolish—battling for this one woman against common sense, not to mention rejection?

"I have the feeling that you don't expect to lose."

"No, Abbie, I don't. I don't take risks unless the odds are in my favor."

"And what makes you think the odds are in your favor this time?"

"Number one," he ticked off on his fingers. "I know you want me wildly and passionately."

"Modest, aren't we?"

"And number two—I spent years working on oil rigs in the most forsaken spots of South America, passing the time by playing cards. I'm a damned good card player."

"No."

"No, what?"

"No, I'm not going to take up your challenge. Marshall and I can manage just fine despite your obnoxious presence. Good night, Mr. Strawhand," she finished with the slam of her door.

The next day, dressed in a stunning black panne velvet sheath, she felt ready to take on Cody. Aggressive men she knew how to handle. Or should have.

But Cody put her through the same routine as the day before, ignoring her haughty looks and condescending smiles. He began the day by suggesting a champagne brunch. Then it was a celebrity tennis tournament at noon, followed by a classy lunch and a tour of the strip. When Cody went to hail a cab to take them back to the jai alai games at the hotel, Marshall put his arm about her waist and said, "You know, I have the distinct impression that I'm not the only one interested in you, Abbie."

She didn't pretend ignorance. "You mean Cody."

He grinned. "Something like that."

"I—I think he'll probably go on to L.A. tomorrow."

Marshall kissed her on the temple. "I value his friendship, but I would also like to value this time with you—alone."

But Cody obviously didn't intend to give the two of them that chance. At one point in the jai alai games, during the furious yelling and wagering on the players, Cody leaned over and said next to her ear, "I'm losing patience, Abbie. If you don't tell him about our child, I will."

She kept her eyes on the handball court below. "I'll deny it."

"I think you have too much integrity for that."

Her gaze swerved upward to Cody's dark one. "All right, you win. But I need to tell him when I think the time is right."

"No, we'll tell him tonight. I'm damned tired of this charade."

They left the jai alai game for dinner at an elegant and intimate Italian restaurant, full of lush greenery and statuary, with a massive canvas mural depicting the splendor and romance of Venice. Seventeeth-century armchairs graced well-spaced tables draped with red linen cloths topped by gossamer ecru lace cloths. But Abbie was unappreciative of the opulence. Dreading the inevitable confrontation later, she drank freely from her crystal glass of Italian red wine but barely tasted her meal.

"You don't like your veal shanks?" Marshall asked in concern.

She glanced at Cody. His eyes challenged hers; then his gaze dropped to her lips, grazing them with a caress she could almost feel. Damn his arrogance. He was openly seducing her! "I'm not that hungry," she murmured.

Later they gambled, but she drank more than she wagered. She should tell both men to go to hell, she thought, mentally cursing her weakness. She shouldn't let Cody dominate her emotions,

her thoughts. This Abbie wasn't the strong, independent woman she had wanted to discover.

The croupier raked in her hard-earned ten-
dollar bill, and she lifted another glass of vodka
from the waitress's tray. Afterward, when the
three of them caught yet another show, each time
she lifted her goblet of champagne her gaze met
Cody's mocking eyes across the glass's rim.

Soon. Soon she would have to tell Marshall the
truth.

As they returned through the overflowing casino en route to their rooms, a page in red livery
passed by, calling out Marshall's name. Marshall
summoned him, and the page said, "Telephone,
sir."

Marshall tipped the young man and crossed to
the bank of telephones nearest the elevator.
Abbie waited uneasily next to Cody. His arm
circled her waist, pulling her to him. With the
bright chandelier spilling its gossamer glow over
the lobby and making the red-felt walls shift and
sway, she unwillingly accepted his support. His
head bent over hers. "No backing out, Abbie."

Her mouth tightened. "I'll tell Marshall, but
only because you're right. He's entitled to know
—which does not, however, entitle you to any
further claim on me."

Cody lowered his head, his mouth lipping the
delicate rim of her ear. "I would like to claim you
right here and now . . . to lay you down across
one of those—"

"Stop it!"

His fingers played with her ribs, tantalizing the skin just below her breasts. "Stop what?"

"What you're doing," she breathed. "What you're saying."

When she saw Marshall replace the telephone receiver, she pulled away from Cody, but placed her palm on the wall to steady her dangerously tilting legs. Marshall wore a scowl when he returned. "Bad news?" Cody asked.

"My ex-wife. She slipped in the tub and broke both hips. She's hospitalized, in traction."

"I'm sorry to hear that," Abbie murmured.

He ran a hand through his sun-bleached hair. "Can't say I'm that sorry. But the hell of it is that there's no one to care for my daughter. I need to fly to Oklahoma and bring her back with me." He took Abbie's hand. "Would you mind flying back tomorrow without me, Abbie?"

"Of course not."

"I can telephone the agency to have someone pick you up at the airport."

"No need," Cody said. "I can fly you back."

"What about your art deal in L.A.?" Abbie demanded.

His glance mocked her. "I can postpone it."

"How kind of you."

"Look," Marshall said, his gray eyes moving from Cody to her. "It's obvious that this is a three-way affair. This will give us all some time to do some thinking."

A wave of red washed over Abbie's face. "Marshall, let me explain what—"

He put his arm over her shoulder and kissed her on the temple. "It's all right, Abbie. No explanation needed. Cody, take good care of her."

Cody's lips curled in a genuine smile. "I intend to, Marshall."

Marshall left them and headed toward the registration desk to check out. Cody ushered Abbie into the waiting elevator. His arm imprisoned her waist, as if he thought she would try to escape. To where? And why, when all her senses were tightly attuned like some microwave saucer toward him? Why did she feel none of that wild fluttering of the heart, that soaring of the senses, for Marshall that she did when she was in Cody's arms?

She tried to remind herself that she had been unwise at seventeen to fall for those same heart-stopping sensations. Surely she was not about to make the same mistake over again. This time she must think rationally, practically, logically—which was difficult when her mind spun hazily from all the alcohol she had imbibed earlier.

The room key she extracted from her beaded clutch purse refused to enter the keyhole in the door of her room. Cody reached around her and steadied her hand. When the door gave, his arm encircled her waist and, still holding her against him, propelled her into the darkened room.

"What do you think you're doing?" she protested in overly precise speech.

One arm continued to hold her waist, pressing her buttocks against him. His free hand slid down to softly rotate against her abdomen. The motion of his palm inched the velvet dress above her knees, but no modesty signaled her of the danger. All her senses were lulled by the hand that stroked sensuously ever nearer that part of her that now ached with longing. Her lungs seemed to freeze; her head drooped forward with the weakness that suddenly possessed her. Strong teeth nipped gently at her nape as he muttered, "Exactly what I told Marshall—I intend to take care of you."

Abbie tried to twist free of the arm that he had wrapped beneath her breast, but Cody only anchored her more tightly against the wall of his chest. Her buttocks only pressed more fully against him in her futile effort to free herself. Her feet wriggled inches above the floor and one of her shoes dropped off.

"Cody . . . no!" But her voice seemed muffled by her wildly beating heart.

He crossed to the bed, yet did not release her; rather he settled her knees on its edge, still keeping her imprisoned with his arm. He held her thus while his lips branded kisses along the back of her neck. A strange lassitude settled its magic web over her.

His free hand released the clasp that bound her hair, and he buried his face in its fragrant mass. "Abbie," he rasped, "I want you so."

She trembled against him. "Cody, it won't work . . . it . . . ." Her words trailed away as his fiery kisses followed along the V created by the gradual opening of her zipper.

"I've damned myself a thousand times for loving you," he whispered. "Don't stop my loving now."

She didn't; she gave herself up to his embrace. Her hand went up to cup the head that nuzzled her now bare shoulder, her fingers curling in the thick, luxuriant hair.

His hand slid beneath her bunched dress and slipped up her leg to palm the delta of her thighs. A tortured sigh escaped her parted lips. Her head fell back against his shoulder. His fingers insinuated themselves beneath the elastic band of her panty hose but refrained from dipping lower to the spot that he had set afire. "I want to hear you say it . . . say you want me, too."

She nodded.

"Say it," he insisted, his hands anchoring her against him.

"Cody," she whispered when he raised his head. "Make me feel like a woman again."

He withdrew his hand and gently turned her to face him. His lips took hers in a strangely tender kiss, and she fitted her mouth to his. Her arms wrapped about his neck. Gently he levered her to the mattress. He kissed first one lid closed, next the other; then he deserted her. In the silence of the room she heard the hiss of his zipper. The waiting was unbearable.

The bedside lamp flared, and she saw reflected above her the smoky image of a woman caught in sensuous abandon. One knee was slightly raised; her dress hem rode high on her thighs and the neckline slipped below her shoulders. Her hair spread over the mauve bedcovers like spilled champagne. She blinked, willing away the lethargy of the alcohol, willing away the vision above her. But the woman was real. Slowly her fingers inched up to her parted lips, as if she didn't quite believe that the enraptured woman in the mirror above was she.

Then Cody's coppery reflection overshadowed hers. Through the fan of her lashes she watched as he bent over her. Openly she studied the beauty of his corded shoulders, the muscles that enlarged his chest, the taut stomach shadowed lower by the crisp, curling hair. His hands came to rest at either side of her while he studied her bemused expression. After a moment his lips curved in a loving smile. "I like you better this way, Abbie. Unashamed of yourself. Unafraid of me."

She held up her arms to him with an answering smile. "And I like you better this way, my naked savage."

Her hips rose to facilitate the hands that inched her panty hose downward. His fingers caressed the silky smoothness of her calves and thighs before he lowered himself over her. As he held his massive body above hers, his mouth possessed hers in a kiss that was rife with caring and tenderness. Her fingers teased his hard brown nipples, and she was rewarded by a groan against her lips. When his head slipped lower and his tongue polished one pouting nipple, she saw their images imposed above her. She saw her legs, draped over the side of the bed, splayed in abandonment as his cheeks flexed to draw in the fullness of the aureole that dimpled with the love play.

Her stomach contracted at the erotic scene being played out above her. When he knelt on the carpet beside the bed to grasp her knees and rain teasing kisses on the insides of her thighs, the reflections above her blurred as her lids drooped. A sweet ecstasy flowed through her like liquid gold, molten sunlight, melded honey and cream.

Only when he moved up over her did her lids open. Her hands cupped the solid curve of his buttocks to draw him to her. She marveled at the hard musculature that rippled just below the surface of his flesh as he fused with her. Had she known of the deep fulfillment to be found in the sensual giving of love . . . perhaps she could have bridged the gap in her marriage that her husband had been unable to.

"How many years have been wasted," she murmured wistfully. "I wish I had known."

"Then you would not be the exquisite woman I hold beneath me," he said in a voice husky with passion.

His breath tickled the hollow of her shoulder and she laughed. "Must I be beneath? I enjoyed the . . . the last ride you gave me."

His teeth nipped the soft skin of her shoulder. "I can remedy that."

He caught her in the small of her back, rolling her over with him so that she found herself astride. An intense exhilaration swept over her as she rode him again. Once, as he stroked her breasts, her head fell back and she saw the exotic motions reproduced in the mirrors above. The erotic sight aroused her even more, but when she would have undulated her hips, he caught her waist with a laugh. "Slow down, Abbie," he said and wrestled her onto her back again. "We've got all night."

All night it was. Or, at least, so it seemed. Once she awoke to find herself ensconced in his arms. Another time he awoke her as he brushed back the skein of hair that had fallen across her face. She smiled at him tentatively. "I'm afraid you'll be sore tomorrow," he said.

"It's already tomorrow," she said, snuggling closer to the warmth of his body. "And I don't hurt."

Her fingers followed the whorls of crisp hair that matted his nipples and abdomen, and his hand caught hers, halting her finger's play. "Shall we try another position?" he teased, his tongue stroking each fingertip.

"Not yet," she laughed. "You've weakened my whole body with your lovemaking."

In the dark he lit a cigarette. She lay next to him, watching its glow in the mirror above them. She found no shame in the reflected beauty of their naked bodies; rather, she gloried in the sight. She had come a long way in the space of only a few months.

"I love the smell of your cigarette," she murmured against the flesh of his chest. "It affects me like fresh coffee in the morning and the bittersweet smell of sagebrush after a rain."

And she loved him. It was a revelation. But the image of him ruffling Robert's hair, covering Miss Halliburton's head with his bandana, laughing at her from across the flame in the firepit—these images superimposed themselves over the two entwined above her.

"Abbie?"

"Hmmmm?"

"What happens now?"

Her leg, scissored between his thighs, shifted and stirred. Her gaze met his in the mirror overhead, but in the haze of smoke she couldn't read his eyes. "We go back to Kaibeto."

"You know that's not what I'm asking."

She steeled herself. "Then tell me."

"Your muscles are tensing beneath my hand," he said, massaging the fleshy area of her arm, "which tells me that I don't have to explain myself."

"Are you asking if I'll marry you?"

He blew a swirl of smoke. Marriage was what he had intended since that first time in the mill house; no, perhaps he had wanted it all along, marriage to this one irresistible, exquisite woman. He needed her warmth and love to make him whole, to blot out the emptiness that was his life without her. He loved her wildly. And that love made him feel terribly vulnerable, a feeling he had not allowed himself since childhood. So he said nothing of that love. Instead, he said, "I don't want our child born a bastard."

"May I have a cigarette, please?"

He reached for the pack and shook a cigarette out. Leaning over her, he placed it between her lips and touched his cigarette to hers. Past the glow, her eyes locked with his. She felt as if she were drowning in the inky depths. The old fear haunted her. She would strangle in the depths of his consuming love.

"I can't." She rushed on. "I've explained this before, Cody. Please, please try to understand me."

He ground out the cigarette in the ceramic ashtray on the nightstand. "I understand that you're afraid of making commitments."

The cigarette left a bad taste in her mouth. She sat up and stubbed hers out, too, in the ashtray next to her. Her hand was trembling. You've handled difficult situations with ease before. This one is no different, she told herself.

"I'm not afraid of making commitments," she said in the monotonous voice of a tour guide. "I just don't *want* to make a commitment. There's a difference. Is that so hard to understand?"

He uncoiled himself and rolled to a sitting position, grasping her upper arms to push her prone on the bed again. His hands pinned her there. "I think I do understand." She shivered at the brutal tone in his voice. "You don't have the fortitude it would take to live out the rest of your life in anything less than a mansion, do you?"

"That's not so." The way he was looking at her, the flicker of hope that shaded the grim lines of his face—she used the last weapon she had. "It's just that a half-breed child deserves better than to end his life hanging himself from some showerhead."

His hands tightened on her arms, his fingers digging into her flesh. "You selfish bitch," he grated. He shoved himself away from her and sat looking at her with his Indian's inscrutable gaze. "Why don't you just destroy our child? It would make everything easier for you."

She turned her head away. Tears clouded her eyes. "I—I couldn't do that . . . I wouldn't do that."

In one smooth movement he rose from the bed. He crossed to the window, jerking the plush velvet-lined drapes apart. The city's bright neon lights lit up the night sky like sunlight, silhouetting the powerful lines of his body. Pressing his forehead and palms against the glass, he kept his back to her. The muscles in his back flickered like a bull's beneath a cattle prod. She was half-afraid he would smash a fist through the window. When he spoke his voice was hoarse with contempt.

"I was right from the start. I knew it that first day when I touched your lily-white palms and saw your mannequin's smile. You're nothing but an empty shell, lady."

A rage, as red and hot as wildfire, swept through her. "Take a good look at your reflection in the window, Cody Strawhand," she cried. "You're afraid to face life . . . real life. And you won't find life hiding out at Kaibeto! You're as much of an empty shell as you call me!"

When he said nothing, she sprang from the bed

and flew at him. Her fists pounded ineffectually on the broad sweep of his back. "Do you think I want to live like some squaw in a hogan with you?" she lashed out.

He whirled and grabbed her wrists. "What makes you think you have the guts and grit to?" He shoved her away from him. "The Indian squaw you talk about is more of a woman than you could ever hope to be."

Chapter 11

DOROTHY GOLDMAN POKED HER HEAD THROUGH the classroom doorway. Abbie halted in mid-sentence and looked up. "It's Miss Halliburton," the old woman said. "She wants to see you in her office."

Abbie stilled the uneasy tightening in her lungs. It was probably nothing. Just because she had spent a miserable Easter vacation, just because the weather had turned worse with snow threatening—incredible for the first week of April —just because Robert was still sulking at the failure of his father to come at Easter—all that didn't necessarily mean that the disastrous trend would continue.

Yet she held little hope that things were going to get any better. The stormy scene with Cody three days earlier had left a bad taste in her mouth and a worse pain in her heart. Why did loving someone have to be so painful and difficult? She had returned to Flagstaff alone, as was getting to be her habit. The scene with Cody had made her more determined than ever to prove— not only to herself but to him also—that she was capable of being a good teacher, that there was more to her than an empty shell.

She dismissed the class for recess in the gym, since the weather was so wretched, and walked with Dorothy down the hall to the principal's office. Dorothy chattered nervously about her retirement, which was coming up in May. "Only seven more weeks, then I don't have to answer to the Dragon Lady or anyone else. I can't imagine . . ."

Abbie couldn't imagine what she herself would do if she lost her job at Kaibeto. Teaching jobs were scarce, and especially for a teacher who was also an unwed mother. A mother at thirty-seven . . . impossible. But she wanted to be with the child. The Indian boarding school system would allow her to keep the child in the compound with her. And she would be surrounded by the Indian women, who were famed for their love of children. They even paid somewhat better than the average school system.

There were many reasons for retaining her job with the BIA school beyond the necessity to prove Cody wrong. Dear God, don't let Miss Halliburton find some small infraction to use against me now, she prayed.

At the office counter, Dorothy deserted her. Abbie walked on past to the principal's door and knocked. In that one moment the awful suspicion occurred that perhaps Cody had arranged, through his father, to put pressure on the BIA to have her fired. Would he really do such a thing? Hadn't he told her he could be relentless? Hadn't she experienced a sample of his relentlessness in Las Vegas? Yet she knew that this time he was finished with her.

Her knees began to wobble, as if they were held together with sponge rather than cartilage. At Miss Halliburton's bidding, she forced herself to open the door. "Do come in," the woman snapped impatiently.

Abbie complied, taking a seat opposite the letter-covered desk. Miss Halliburton held an open folder before her. She didn't lift her gaze but continued to read. Abbie had the satisfaction of noting that the woman's wig was slightly askew. A harried morning?

That doesn't bode well for me, Abbie thought with a sinking heart.

At last Miss Halliburton looked up. "Well! It seems that you have gone and done it again."

Abbie's heart thudded and fell. "Done what?"

"Attracted the attention of the BIA in Gallop."

Abbie's heart ceased its thudding altogether. "What did I do this time?" she managed to ask.

The principal's dun gray eyes narrowed, her mouth pinched until the lips were invisible. "The beads you had the children make and sell . . ."

"Yes?" *Oh, please just get this torturous waiting over with.*

Miss Halliburton jabbed a gnarled finger at a place on the file folder. "The BIA is upset that you did not file for a vendor's license, a commercial tax number."

Oh, dear! She had forgotten to put in a request through the BIA. And she had assured Miss Halliburton that she had taken care of everything. "Yes?"

The principal slapped the folder closed. "I'm afraid that you are officially on probation, Mrs. Dennis. I have to tell you that the BIA has been debating whether to renew the fall portion of your contract."

Abbie's eyes closed. She felt so weak that she didn't know if she would have the strength even to open her lids again.

"Fortunately, I, uh, convinced them to offer you a position at the boarding school at Ganado. I felt that perhaps you might have fewer problems at a different school. Your room and board here will, of course, be paid through August."

It could be worse. Abbie opened her eyes. She might as well get the worst over with now. "I'm expecting a baby in August, Miss Halliburton."

"Well?"

Abbie blinked. "You heard what I said?"

"What do you expect—congratulations?" Miss Halliburton tossed the folder into a wire basket. A genuine smile cracked her principal's mask. "Women have babies all the time. Treat it just like a bad cold, and I'm sure you'll come through just fine. Now out! I've got work to do."

Like the crystalline snowflakes that continued to blanket the red earth, Abbie drifted back to her empty classroom in a state of relief. Not only had she retained her teacher's position, thanks to Miss Halliburton's intervention, but she would be working at a boarding school where she would not have to worry about running into Cody.

Her relief was slightly diluted when Becky rushed breathlessly to the door. "In the gym—I turned around—and he was gone!"

Abbie dropped the paper she was grading. "What? Who?"

The frazzled Becky ran a hand through her stringy hair. "At recess. Robert. He's gone."

Robert. Of course. "You'll just have to look for him, Becky."

"What if Dragon Lady finds out?" she wailed. "He disappeared when I was supposed to be watching him."

Abbie shrugged. Robert wasn't her responsibility this time. The child probably detested her as much as she did him. Besides, in a few weeks she would never have to wipe the spittle from her face again. "Just brazen it out when she calls you on the carpet."

Becky groaned. "I don't even know where to start looking."

"Try the trading post or the old mission." Let Becky deal with Cody and Robert this time.

"I don't know where it is," she whined. "And

how would I get there? I can't walk in this weather. And my car's battery is as cold as an ice cube."

Abbie swore beneath her breath. "All right, I'll go for Robert. I'll use the Jeep. Besides, I think I know where he is. Cover for me."

She was wrong. She realized it immediately when she went to the shed to get the Jeep—and found both the wagon and the burros missing. Robert had never used the wagon to go to Cody's. Pulling her rabbit jacket tighter about her, she went to the corral gates. There, out of the protective lee of the shed, the wind blustered around her. Pushing her hair from her face, she searched the snow before her. Wagon tracks. Her gaze followed the path the wagon wheels had rutted. The tracks ran north. Her gaze lifted. Dominating the northern horizon, Navajo Mountain loomed—and beckoned.

The old Jeep demanded that she pump its pedal several times before its engine decided to deliver a coughing wheeze and kick in. Abbie whispered a prayer and shifted into reverse. It shot out of the shed backward and charged down one of the corral's mesquite posts. Her heart sickened at the crack of the wood, but she jammed the gears back into first and bolted on past the shed and out of the school grounds.

The snowflakes she had thought so marvelous were now headache number one-hundred-and-five. They were falling faster and threatened to soon obliterate the tracks. How long a start had Robert gotten on her? Half an hour? The tracks angled off into one of the canyon mazes that she and the children had taken on the seed-gathering outing. When the shoulder of the road began to drop away precipitously, she kept her gaze trained to the ground immediately ahead of the Jeep.

She began muttering to herself to keep up her courage. Why couldn't the Jeep have been provided with a canvas top? It was getting killingly cold! She really ought to turn back and notify the principal or the BIA or the tribal police or the highway patrol. Or the president of the United States.

Let the rescue teams do their own jobs. But a nagging voice muttered back that the wagon tracks would be completely covered by the time a search party set out. The tracks were already faint as it was.

All at once, as she topped a rise, the Jeep slid on the slick snow and tilted precariously to the left, where the bank seemed to ease off into oblivion. She screamed and shut her eyes. Her hands held onto the steering wheel in a death grip. The Jeep lurched sideways and shuddered. A crunching noise rent the quiet of the canyon— and then there was silence again. Warily Abbie opened her eyes. The Jeep had come to a stop against the trunk of a medium-size pine that was now bowed dangerously, as if it were about to give.

Carefully Abbie pulled her feet up beneath her in the seat and, afraid even to take a breath, began to edge herself over the side of the door.

The pine started to vibrate at her merest movement, then held steady. She slid out over the side.
The snow wisped beneath her shoes. She looked
up the road that disappeared into white shadows
faintly laced with the gray green of pine and cedar
and juniper. No sign of Robert. She turned to
look back down the road she had come along. It
was a long way back on foot. And this time she
couldn't take her heels off.

She stood there shivering as the light wind
playfully flipped her skirt and ran tickling fingers
up her legs. Robert was no longer her problem.
She was leaving Kaibeto. Rescue parties were
good—better than she—at this sort of thing. With
his Indian luck he had probably made it all the
way to Navajo Mountain by now.

She stepped out onto the snow-packed road—
and turned her steps north toward Navajo Mountain. Damn the little brat.

Her heels sank into the snow with each step she
took. This was sheer folly. She wrapped her arms
about her. Another two hours and the sun would
be setting behind the mesas. It would be cold and
dark. Would Becky think to tell anyone that she
and Robert were gone? Probably not. The girl
would blithely assume that she had found Robert.
Had she not as much as told Becky that she knew
where he was? And Dalah wouldn't miss Robert
from the dormitory until later that evening.

Her shoes were soaked, her feet frozen. Worse,
it was getting difficult to follow the wagon tracks.
Sometimes tens of yards went by before she
picked up the trail again. The wind whistled down

the canyons, sharp and hard. If only she had gloves. And earmuffs . . . and boots . . . and snowpants . . . and a Jeep . . . and . . . Damn, but it was cold. She should turn back now before it got any darker. Robert was probably sitting inside a warm hogan, toasting his feet before the firepit.

The tracks disappeared altogether. She kept walking. Maybe they would show up soon. Nothing. Maybe she had missed them. Maybe they had turned off down one of those narrow side canyons. She stopped and half turned, unsure what she should do. In that deep labyrinth of canyons, with the snow falling all about and silencing the world under its white blanket, she felt terribly alone—and more than a little scared. A person could freeze to death in a matter of hours out here.

She started walking north again, toward the mountain. She supposed that she should try to find some sort of shelter. Underbrush, a recess in the rocky walls. Hadn't she read somewhere that if no shelter could be found one ought to dig a cave in the snow? She shivered just thinking about her fingers clawing through the ice. They were so numb that she probably wouldn't feel a thing.

She halted. The tracks. She had picked them up again. They were deeper—and veered suddenly off to the edge. "No," she whispered.

Her steps lagged, her legs unwilling to take her any nearer the precipice. Her hands clenched as she forced her faltering feet to the edge. She looked down. It wasn't quite a sheer drop-off, more like a steep, rocky incline salted with scrubby trees. Even so, dizziness swept over her. She closed her eyes and slowly sank to her knees and safe ground. When she looked again, her feeling of vertigo wasn't quite as bad. With the snow falling like a gauze curtain, it was difficult to distinguish any distinct forms. She was going to have to climb down the side of the bluff.

She closed her eyes again. She couldn't do it. Maybe the tracks were old, from another wagon at another time. She knew she was stalling, losing precious time. "Robert!" she called.

A moment passed, and then she thought she heard his voice, muffled, remote. Then she distinctly heard him shout some Navajo word. Her sigh was a mixture of relief and dread. He was alive. But she was going to have to get him. She rocked back and forth on her knees. I can't. I can't climb down that bluff. They can't expect that of me.

She wouldn't. Robert had done this to himself. It was *his* fault. Her job didn't include mountain-climbing and search and rescue. She didn't even have to work at Kaibeto anymore. No one would blame her if she couldn't get to him. She had done her best, hadn't she?

She took off her heels. She had to be half an idiot.

She thought about all the times when she had disdained the careless clothing styles of the other teachers, and wished now that she had on something half as serviceable. Oh, for one pants suit.

Or a dirty pair of sneakers. She was learning a lot . . . but perhaps too late.

Feet first, she edged over the side. With the stones serving as footholds, she inched her way downward. She kept her eyes tightly shut. At some points she found she could half stand where the incline jutted out, and then it was back to her knees. Once her foot lost its toehold and the rock gashed its way up her shinbone. All she could think about were the torn panty hose . . . until she slipped the next time.

"Robert!" she screamed as her hands grabbed wildly for anything to hold on to.

She started tumbling. Something—her fingers clawed about the rock. Her feet thrashed futilely for a toehold. Nothing. She looked down. Through the trees—past the oddly tilted wagon— she could see, far below, a small stream, its line of blue glistening against the blanket of snow that looked gray with the approaching darkness.

A wave of dizziness swept over her. She closed her eyes again. For a moment she wasn't even certain which way was up, and the disorientation caused her fingers to weaken their hold. Oh, God, help. Help me, she prayed.

Tears squeezed from her eyes. Her breath came in staccato bursts. Her hands were gradually losing their grip. Her nails—there were none. They were torn away. How much longer could she hold on?

She saw a scruffy sapling three or four feet to her left and another couple of feet below her. She held little hope that it would bear her weight. If it didn't . . . She risked a dizzy glance downward. If it didn't, the fall would be a long one, with only the trees to break her plunge. But if the sapling held, larger rocks and trees zigzagged a path down the slight plateau where the wagon lay tilted against the pine.

Despite the frigid temperature, perspiration broke out on her temples and upper lip. She really had no alternative. She had to leap those few feet quickly before the last of her strength ebbed. *I can't!* Tears of frustration and helplessness trickled down her cheeks to mix with the snowflakes.

Slowly she began to draw from a reservoir of unrealized, untapped strength. Forcing her mind to go as numb as her toes and fingers, she started swaying her feet and legs, like someone gathering speed on a swing to climb higher. One hand slipped. She lunged then. Her hands desperately and blindly flailed the air for that insignificant sapling. The rough, cylindrical trunk skimmed her palms. Her fingers locked around it. The trunk dipped and bowed—and she held her breath and prayed.

The pine's swaying subsided. Stretching her legs and toes, Abbie could feel the solid ledge of stone just below her. If she released her grip on the pine, could she keep her balance on the ledge? There was no choice, was there?

Her heart thudding like a cottonwood drum, she loosened her hold and dropped. Her numb feet, shocked by the jarring, gave way and she fell to her knees. Afraid to move for fear of toppling backward, she hugged the rocky wall. When she

saw the tiny crimson trickling down the limestone
wall, she realized that she must have scraped her
forehead in the drop.

No time to worry about that. The worst of the
descent was over. Cautiously she worked her way
down, using the tree trunks and outcroppings of
rocks like rungs on a ladder. Finally she made it
to the plateau. Twenty yards from the wagon she
sank to her knees, weakened more by her fear
than the effort. When she looked up, Robert was
scooting toward her, dragging one leg behind
him, as if it were broken.

She was so relieved to see him that she snapped
out, "If you dare spit at me, Robert Tsinnijinnie,
I swear I'll break your other leg."

Sitting, they faced each other. Robert's eyes
were like coals against the backdrop of snow. "I
suppose it's a truce?" she asked when he made no
belligerent motion.

No reply.

She looked around them, assessing their situation. "The burros? Where are they?"

He pointed to the chasm below. A brown lump
stood out against the snow. She started shaking
all over again. That could have been her. She
couldn't go to pieces now.

"Both of the burros?"

His brown finger aimed like an arrow to the
north, where the plateau narrowed to little more
than a ledge again. The other burro had apparently escaped. So much for hope of a burro ride
back. With Robert hurt there was no way the two
of them could climb back up that bluff. And she

wasn't certain that she had the courage to do it again, anyway. It almost seemed easier to let the blessing of the freezing cold hush them into painless, permanent sleep than to attempt that nightmare ascent.

However . . . For the first time she smiled. If the burro had escaped by way of that narrow path, perhaps they could, too. She turned to Robert. "Look, Robert, the snow will soon cover our tracks." Did he understand her? She doubted it, but it helped her retain her sanity to talk. "If we can make it back to the road, there's hope that the school will send out a search party."

A futile hope, since they probably wouldn't realize that she and Robert were missing until later that night. And how many canyons would have to be searched before they were found? They could freeze to death by then. But she couldn't—she *wouldn't*—sit there and wait for death's wings to flap over the two of them.

She pushed herself erect and staggered. Had her feet fallen off? A quick glance reassured her that they were still there. She started giggling and broke off sharply. "Let's go, Robert." She bent and slipped an arm under his shoulders. If he balked now, she would cry. He didn't. He balanced on one leg and wrapped an arm about her waist.

His questioning glance prompted her into movement, movement that sent jabs of needlelike pain into the soles of her feet. Leaning into each other, the two of them hobbled along the narrowing ledge. With a grim smile Abbie thought that they looked like contestants in a potato sack race.

For a while she was galvanized by the hope of making it back to the top. Robert's weight, her numb feet and hands, were forgotten in the struggle to put yard after yard behind them. But her hopes were shattered when they edged around a bend of the wall to find that the path had narrowed to a mere goat trail. There was little room to do more than place one foot in front of the other. It was an impossibility for Robert, with his injured leg.

And for her? Her feet had no feeling in them. Even if she could manage to crawl, her sense of balance was decimated by fatigue. With the certainty that comes hand in hand with desperation, she knew that she would never make it to the top, but would join the carcass of the unfortunate burro below.

"And we were so close to reaching the top," she murmured, too tired even to cry. She sank down with Robert and laid her head against the wall of rock. She wouldn't look into the abyss yawning below, but she did slide a glance at the boy beside her. His swarthy face had a pallor beneath it. His dark eyes were dull, his bowlike mouth pinched with the pain in his leg, but no fear etched his face; it held only a complacent acceptance of the situation.

She slipped an arm around him and pulled his head into the crook of her shoulder. "You're one hell of a kid, Robert Tsinnijinnie."

Watching the snow swirl about them, she

thought of her own boys. How she loved them; how she missed those years of their childhood . . . and recalled again, with a faint smile, those precious moments of bedtime prayers. The thought of bedtime reminded her of just how sleepy she was. She knew that she wasn't supposed to sleep, that the two of them should keep active, keep moving. But where? Retrace those tortured steps back down to the plateau? She shook her head and closed her eyes. It wasn't worth it.

Thoughts of Cody, and the child she carried, invaded her comfortable lethargy. She would never hold the child to her breast. And Cody . . . she knew now that she loved him beyond all else . . . beyond herself. Yet if she had given their love a chance, would that desperate need to discover herself have resurfaced one day to smother that love? She would never know now, would she? She really couldn't think clearly with the drowsy lassitude that was settling over her like the snow.

Her head bobbled. Cement sacks bounced inside, just like the morning after she had drunk so much at Cody's house.

"You little idiot. You stupid fool. Damn you to hell."

Like an infant that preferred the womb to the cold, howling world without, Abbie closed her eyes all the more tightly. She was reluctant to face whatever it was that was intruding on her warm cocoon. But the stabbing ache in her feet and

hands, the jarring of her head, were becoming
more acute by the second. Her lids opened slightly. She was peering, head first, into the greedy
mouth of the gorge far below.

"No!" she groaned and tried to push herself
away from that vast emptiness waiting below for
her.

The sharp slap against her buttocks brought her
up short. "For God's sake, Abbie, cut it out,"
Cody's voice growled, "or we'll both be doing
free falls."

"How . . . what? . . ." She struggled to coa-
lesce her scattered senses. After another moment
of excruciating jarring, she realized that she was
thrown over Cody's shoulder, that he was negoti-
ating that perilous path. An impossibility. She
twisted her head to see, and he landed another
blow across her rear. "I said don't move."

She froze at his command. Incredibly, he was
climbing the foot-wide path by hauling on a rope
that stretched somewhere upward out of sight.

She heard him chuckle and demanded, "How
can you laugh at a time like this?"

"I was thinking . . . for the umpteenth time
. . . what a delightful rear you have. The one opportunity . . . I have to fondle it—" his breathing was labored, and he paused to inhale—
"without you interfering . . . and I need both my
hands for the task at hand."

"Thank God."

"Thank the burro that returned to the shed.
. . . That's when we knew you were missing.

Otherwise hours could have passed before we started looking."

"And I thought burros were dumb." Her breath whooshed from her lungs as her body jolted with one of Cody's rough strides. When her breath returned, she asked, "Robert?"

"In the pickup. He's broken a thighbone."

Her relief came out in an audible sigh. Then Cody's foot slid, and she screamed, certain that the two of them were going over the edge.

Cody's hands slipped on the rope, then held. He started working his way back up the pebbled path, hauling the two of them ever upward. She was afraid even to draw a breath, much less open her eyes, until it seemed that Cody was walking upright. Then the hinges of a door squeaked, and a rush of toasted air swept over her. She opened her eyes to find Cody shoving her into his pickup. The motor was running, filling the cab with heat. Next to her, Robert, half unconscious from the combined effects of the cold and the pain itself, stirred on the seat, where he had slumped to one side. She looked around for Cody. He stood at the tailgate, unknotting the hemp rope that he had used in the rescue from the bumper.

She and Robert were going to live after all! With the realization she started to shiver as feeling returned to her limbs again. Inexplicably she began to cry in silent little gasps.

Cody opened the pickup door and swung into the cab. "What the hell are you doing?"

She had no breath to answer him, only sobbing

hiccoughs as she buried her face in her hands. The aftershock hit her and she cried copiously, uncontrollably.

The same emotional reaction to Abbie's safety wrapped cold tentacles about Cody, but it took a different form. "You little idiot." He began to curse again, quietly, unemotionally and steadily, as he shifted the engine into forward and drove back down the canyon. "You selfish little fool. Why couldn't you have stayed in Pennsylvania where you belonged? But, no . . . you just had to prove what a woman you were, no matter how much it disrupted other lives."

"You have no right to say that!" She dropped her bloodied, ragged hands from her face and looked at him with a face ravaged by tears.

He didn't take his eyes from the dark road, lit only by the pickup's headlights. "But it's true, isn't it?" he ground out between clenched teeth. "You came here looking for amusement— entertainment—any diversion from the boredom of your *haute monde.*"

Robert stirred, awakened by the virulent tension that vibrated in the cab. But Abbie was unaware of anything but the pain caused by Cody's charge. "No, no!" she cried out. "I thought I would find real life here at Kaibeto. I thought I would find *myself!*"

"And did you?" he grated. "Did you find real life at Kaibeto? Did you find the real you?"

"No," she sobbed bitterly. Her shoulders shook with her vehemence. "I was wrong, thinking I would find myself here. I'm leaving the reservation, do you hear! I'm going back to Pennsylvania, where I belong."

Abbie laid the folded sweater in the suitcase with the rest of her meager belongings . . . and one of the beaded necklaces made by the children. Miss Halliburton had insisted that she take it after Abbie had informed the older woman that she was leaving the reservation.

The doctor had recommended a few days of rest and recuperation, but Miss Halliburton had told her to take off the weeks remaining in the term. It was then that Abbie had announced that she was giving up her position at Kaibeto. "It was the mountains and the gorges that got to me finally," Abbie finished with a smile that rang hollow with self-mockery.

"And the baby you carry?" Miss Halliburton asked. "What will your husband—former husband—say?"

Abbie shrugged. "I don't really care. I'm not going back to him, only to the life that I'm familiar with. I don't belong out here, Miss Halliburton."

"I'd say you're one gutsy lady."

It was the first compliment Abbie had received from the woman. Perhaps the principal wasn't such a dragon after all. Why did she have to realize certain truths when it was too late? Abbie wondered.

"Not too gutsy. I'm scared silly just thinking

about trying to earn a living and raise a baby alone. But other women do it. Besides, in a way, I'm looking forward to the challenge."

It would take her mind off other things. Off her failure as a teacher. Off Cody. Off her love for him and for continued desire for him. Now that he had awakened the sleeping woman within her, what would she do with the rest of her life? Read romantic books to sublimate these new, unsettling feelings? Cody's last words had killed all hope for anything else.

They had been waiting outside Tuba City's emergency clinic for the doctor to finish setting the cast on Robert's leg. Cody, his hands jammed in his jeans, his back to her as he stood at the dust-filmed window, had said in a low, brusque voice, "Get out of my life, Abbie Dennis." Only then had he turned to look at her. Really look at her. Below the bandana his eyes were hard and piercing. "Get out and don't come back."

She had looked away. "There's nothing to bring me back," she had said in a toneless voice.

And it was true, she thought as she clumsily closed the lid on the leather-bound suitcase with hands that were wrapped in gauze and tape. In the four days following the snowstorm she had had enough time to rethink her decision to leave, and the unpleasant facts she faced had not changed her mind. Cody's contempt, Robert's dislike, her teaching career that was nothing more than one fiasco after another—she had failed utterly, miserably at Kaibeto.

She looked around the apartment for anything

she might have missed. There was still time to say good-bye to her students. But that was another painful situation she couldn't bring herself to face. Better to wait in the school office for Marshall to arrive. Carrying her suitcase in one hand, her coat thrown over her other arm, she walked across the school grounds. The snow had melted, leaving the greasewood and broomgrass glistening in the brilliant sunlight that had perversely decided to shine. Beneath the slide, about the corral, between the sidewalk's gaping cracks—everywhere, it seemed—sunflowers suddenly unfolded their gloriously golden petals to usher in the spring.

Yet Abbie's heart was dormant with winter's frost. She set her suitcase down on the school porch's bottom step and turned to survey Kaibeto one last time. Her gaze went to Navajo Mountain. Against a turquoise sky it rose, one magnificent slab of stone. Powerful and enduring, like the Navajo people. She would miss them.

She saw the telltale spiral of dust before she actually heard Marshall's Jeep coming down the road. He pulled up beside her. His gray eyes took in the lovely woman in the white wool suit. "Are you sure?" he asked.

She nodded. She didn't trust herself to speak. He got out of the Jeep and came around to the porch. His hand touched her elbow. "I can still write and tell headquarters to disregard your resignation."

She shook her head. "No." It was all she could manage.

He took her suitcase and opened the door of the Jeep for her. She sat with eyes that stared stonily ahead as they slowly rolled away.

"Wait!" Marshall braked at Abbie's sudden command.

He turned his gaze in the direction she was looking. Robert stood on the steps, his crutches supporting the weight of his thin body. As Abbie watched, he maneuvered the crutches down the three steps, looking for all the world like some unwieldy robot. Frustration showed on his little brown face as he reached the bottom step. Then he dropped the crutches and came hobbling toward her.

"Robert!" she whispered, her throat choked with tears. She flung open the door and ran toward him. She sank to her knees and wrapped her arms about his waist. His own arms encircled her shoulders.

"Shirt." It was all he said. But she knew. She hadn't failed. She started laughing. Robert's childish laughter echoed her own.

She had been determined that she wasn't going to cry, but then, there she was, bawling like a baby, she and Robert both. Brad would have said that she was making a spectacle of herself, but Cody . . . She suspected that he would have had a tear or two in his eyes, as did the people she suddenly glimpsed through blurry eyes standing on the school porch.

Crying and grinning, what a combination they were. Joey Kills the Soldier, Dalah, Linda, Karen

Many Goats, Miss Halliburton, Julie Begay, Dorothy, Becky, Delbert—they were all there.

Marshall touched her shoulder. She looked up into the warm, smiling face. "You'll return to the schoolroom?" he asked.

She came to her feet, still holding Robert's hand. "Not yet. There's something I still have to do. Don't wait for me."

She kissed Robert on the forehead. "I'll come back . . . soon," she told him, and knew that this time he understood her.

She waved at the others, who watched in puzzlement as she turned back and crossed the school grounds toward her apartment. She found what she was looking for on the top shelf of the closet where she had tossed it. She smiled shyly at her reflection in the mirror. With the blanket wrapped around her, she did look like a squaw. A marriage blanket, Cody had called it when he had bundled her in it the night of the windsong ceremony. Would he still want her?

The question echoed in the chambers of her heart with each step that took her closer to the old mission. No fear gripped her, as it used to, when she crossed the narrow foot bridge that spanned Kaibeto Wash . . . only the fear of what Cody would—or would not—do.

The mission's heavy door was open to let in the warming sunshine. The muted pounding told her where he was. She followed the portico that rimmed the courtyard to the clapboard building at the rear. Inside a fire blazed at the forge, highlighting the planes and ridges and hollows of Cody's chiseled face. Naked to the waist, he wielded the hammer against the anvil with a grace that was sensuously masculine. She stood there watching, afraid to move, now that she had come this far.

And she had come far. She had traveled the long road to find the woman within her. She had found Abbie Dennis.

With an Indian's sixth sense, Cody perceived the presence of another in the shed. He halted his hammering of the silver strip and slowly turned to face her. For a long moment he didn't say anything, simply stared at the woman who stood before him, her tawny gold hair draped over the blanket wrapped about her. She was barefooted and his observant eyes noted that her hose had a thin run up one leg.

His eyes gleamed brilliantly against his dark face. "You have made the commitment?"

"Yes." She went to stand before him, dropping the blanket at their feet. "I want to be here at Kaibeto with you."

Still he didn't move. He couldn't. His own fear, a fear such as he had never known as a child, drummed in his head, pounded against his heart. "What happens, Abbie, if that need to find the woman you are, to prove yourself, starts to eat away at you again? Will it erode your love for me, too?"

She cupped the strong line of his jaw in hands that trembled with the love she bore him and looked up into the dark eyes that hungrily searched hers. "I found myself here at Kaibeto, my love," she whispered. "You . . . Robert . . . the others here . . . have shown me the Abbie Dennis who was inside me all along. The conflict in me—trying to be my own woman, wanting to be your woman—is resolved. I can be both. I *am* both."

"And the conflict between our two worlds?" he asked, his voice husky with the anxiety that gnawed at him.

A slow smile danced at the corners of her lips. "You managed to bridge both worlds. Can I, as a woman, do less?" The smile faded to a serious look of pleading. "Oh, Cody, I love your world. I love the tranquility of Kaibeto, the stark, uncluttered beauty of the landscape. I love the challenge of the elements and the people—their humor, their kindness, their honesty and open approach to life. I want to be here at Kaibeto with you."

He encircled her with arms that gleamed with perspiration. His lips made hungry little forays over her face. "Kaibeto can wait," he murmured. "Cambria needs us for a while. It needs our child and our children's children . . . as I need you," he finished, and finally claimed her lips with a kiss that told of his love.

And as he lowered her to the marriage blanket, spread for them on the dirt floor, her own lips and hands told him of her own feelings, as did her whispered words, "Walk in beauty, my love."

Silhouette Intimate Moments

Coming Next Month

Serpent In Paradise by Stephanie James

At first Jase Lassiter had promised Amy paradise, offering her nights of love and days of sheer delight. But then she thought he'd betrayed her and she wondered if paradise would ever be found.

A Season Of Rainbows by Jennifer West

Christopher Reynolds was a genius on the brink of realization—realization that beneath Lauren's cool exterior beat the heart of a woman waiting to be awakened by passion!

Until The End Of Time by June Trevor

The private wilderness of Rafiki was Reed Kincaid's haven, until Elise brought the outside world to his door. He hadn't wanted to love again, but she was woman enough to change his mind.

Tonight And Always by Nora Roberts

Kasey was an anthropologist, but her knowledge of men in general hadn't prepared her for one man in particular: Jordan. Together they did research for his novel, and found something even more precious than knowledge.

Silhouette Intimate Moments

Available Now

Wind Song by Parris Afton Bonds

Abbie went to the reservation school as a teacher, looking for the independent part of herself that she'd never known. She hadn't counted on meeting Cody Strawhand, world-renowned silversmith, and discovering that the independent Abbie was all-too-ready to fall in love.

Island Heritage by Monica Barrie

Real Estate tycoon, Perri Cortland, realized she wanted more than just the purchase of Sophia Island, Krane Elliott's home. She desired his love as well, a desire that turned to desperation.

A Distant Castle by Sue Ellen Cole

Ryan Sagan had been the object of Holly's one childhood crush, but success had marked them both in the intervening years, changing them into opposites that were destined to attract.

Love Everlasting by Möeth Allison

Wall Street Investment Banker, Jay Gatling, helped Libby Dresier turn her cottage cosmetics company into a major competitor in the glitter industry. But, without them realizing it, the competition took on larger dimensions and threatened to keep them apart.

Dear Reader:
Please take a few moments to fill out this questionnaire. It will help us give you more of the Silhouette Intimate Moments you'd like best.

Mail to: **Karen Solem**
Silhouette Books
1230 Ave. of the Americas, New York, N.Y. 10020

1. How did you obtain **WIND SONG?** 9-5

10-1 ☐ **Bookstore**　　　　　　　-6 ☐ **Newsstand**
　-2 ☐ **Supermarket**　　　　　　-7 ☐ **Airport**
　-3 ☐ **Variety/discount store**　　-8 ☐ **Book Club**
　-4 ☐ **Department store**　　　　-9 ☐ **From a friend**
　-5 ☐ **Drug store**　　　　　　　-0 ☐ **Other:**_____
　　　　　　　　　　　　　　　　　　　　　　(write in)

2. How many Silhouette Intimate Moments have you read including this one?
(circle one number) 11- **1 2 3 4**

3. Overall how would you rate this book?
12-1 ☐ **Excellent**　-2 ☐ **Very good**
　-3 ☐ **Good**　-4 ☐ **Fair**　-5 ☐ **Poor**

4. Which elements did you like best about this book?
13-1 ☐ **Heroine**　-2 ☐ **Hero**　-3 ☐ **Setting**　-4 ☐ **Story line**
　-5 ☐ **Love scenes**　-6 ☐ **Ending**　-7 ☐ **Other Characters**

5. Do you prefer love scenes that are
14-1 ☐ **Less explicit than**　　　-2 ☐ **More explicit than**
　　　in this book　　　　　　　　**in this book**
　　　　　　-3 ☐ **About as explicit as in this book**

6. What influenced you most in deciding to buy this book?
15-1 ☐ **Cover**　-2 ☐ **Title**　-3 ☐ **Back cover copy**
　-4 ☐ **Recommendations**　-5 ☐ **You buy all Silhouette Books**

7. How likely would you be to purchase other Silhouette Intimate Moments in the future?
16-1 ☐ **Extremely likely**　　　　-3 ☐ **Not very likely**
　-2 ☐ **Somewhat likely**　　　　-4 ☐ **Not at all likely**

8. Have you been reading . . .
17-1 ☐ **Mostly Silhouette Romances**
　-2 ☐ **Mostly Silhouette Special Editions**
　-3 ☐ **Mostly Silhouette Desires**
　-4 ☐ **Any other romance series**_____
　　　　　　　　　　　　　　(write one in)

9. Please check the box next to your age group.
18-1 ☐ **Under 18**　-3 ☐ **25-34**　　-5 ☐ **50-54**
　-2 ☐ **18-24**　　-4 ☐ **35-49**　　-6 ☐ **55 +**

10. Would you be interested in receiving a romance newsletter? If so please fill in your name and address.

Name_____

Address_____

City_____ State_____ Zip_____

　　　　　　　　　　19___ 20___ 21___ 22___ 23___